Oswald's Project

By
Fiona Law

E
P

Eternal Press
A division of Damnation Books, LLC.
P.O. Box 3931
Santa Rosa, CA 95402-9998
www.eternalpress.biz

Oswin's Project
by Fiona Law

Digital ISBN: 978-1-61572-584-7
Print ISBN: 978-1-61572-585-4
Cover art by: Amanda Kelsey
Edited by: Naomi Clark

To Bronwen, with love

Chapter One

A shadow darted across the top of the old wall clock. Just a flutter of movement. Oswin looked up at once, his fine, straight hair shifting like desert sands across his scalp. He sat riveted, frozen in mid-chew, staring keenly with gray, bespectacled eyes at the clock. It was hideous—a wooden, ornate thing with a pair of cherubs carved at the top—creepy! It had originally hung in the dining room, but recently found its way into the kitchen-diner.

Perhaps, Oswin thought, p*erhaps, Gemma is right about their house.*

This wasn't his house. He was only a guest, a border. He went home for most weekends and all the holidays, only staying here with his cousins and uncle in order to attend a private school. When he first moved in at the beginning of the school year, he thought Gemma had been overreacting, but perhaps...

"Gemma!" he called, letting his spoon fall into his bowl of cereal, and racing up the stairs two at a time. At the top of the landing he paused, ran his fingers through his hair, then marched briskly down the landing to her door.

"Gemma!" he called again, his voice rising to a hoarse squeak. "Open up, it's..."

The door opened a crack and an elegant, white hand shot out, clutching Oswin firmly by the collar and pulling him in. The door shut behind him with hardly a click.

He stood face to face with his cousin, Gemma. She still held onto his collar with one hand and in the other, she held a large, flat brush. It looked like a paddle in her delicate fist.

"Shh!" she hissed, her dark, almond eyes wide and her cheeks flushed in her pale face. She was a pretty little thing, with that elfin look about her and movements that were quick and nervous. She had the sort of rigid posture that ballerinas get.

Gemma waved her brush earnestly towards the door. Oswin pursed his wide lips and nodded, staring earnestly back to show he knew to be quiet, and he turned to open the door. Gemma leapt into his way, landing neatly in front of the door on stocking feet. She spread her scrawny arms and legs out across it, preventing Oswin from opening it.

"But the rules," he said lamely.

"I just want to get to school today without any conversations," whispered Gemma. "I don't feel like all that 'blah...blah...blah!' today."

"Perhaps I should...I could speak to you later..."

"Not you, silly! *Her!*" Gemma indicated to the doorway behind her with a flick of her head and a roll of her eyes. Her rosebud mouth pouted and she frowned determinedly.

"Okay," Oswin replied gently. He understood perfectly and sympathized with her. He stepped back, away from the door—moved over to her dressing table, leaning on its cluttered surface. One or two little bottles toppled over. He avoided looking at the unmade, rumpled bed in front of him by turning to put the bottles up right. Gemma relaxed and began to brush masses of curling, auburn hair, far too thick for her thin frame.

"Well, what is it?" she whispered pleasantly enough, pointing her toes and kicking her ballet shoes under her bed, trying to tidy her room as she finished dressing.

"I was just thinking," began Oswin slowly. He adjusted his specs. Suddenly it all seemed so silly, but he struggled on. "Well, the thing is...I've just seen something rather...peculiar."

Gemma froze in mid stroke, her eyebrows arched, enquiringly. He continued, "I think I saw..."

A door banged, cutting his sentence short and making them both jump.

After a pause Gemma whispered, "That's the bathroom door," and resumed brushing her hair—with faster strokes, now.

"Your Dad?" asked Oswin.

"No. He left over half an hour ago. He popped in to make sure I was up."

"It must be *her*—Beryl—then."

"Good!" Gemma deftly plaited her hair into a thick rope running down her back. A chestnut haze fuzzed above her head like a halo. She shoved her feet, twisting frantically, into her shoes without undoing the buckles. "I've got time for a quick breakfast now," she announced as she fled out the room and down the stairs.

Oswin followed her as far as her doorway and stood looking after her, running his fingers through his hair. He wondered if Gemma rushed about like that to avoid staying still in a house that gave her the creeps, or to avoid being pinned down by her elder sister, Beryl. Or was it a bit of both? He sighed, still pondering the matter, when the door opposite swung open to reveal a large girl, looking much older than her seventeen and three quarter years. She dressed in long layers and dramatic colors. Today's eye blinder was a cyan v-necked jumper, stretched across her generous bust. An unbuttoned waist coat fell alongside a multicolored scarf to below her wide hips. Even her face and nose were long. Apart from the same hair tone and rose-bud mouth, she didn't really resemble her younger sister. Her peepers were small and a watery hazel—nothing like Gemma's deep and soulful eyes.

Oswin stood, blinking stupidly up at Beryl, for a moment. Realizing that his mouth was open, he shut it quickly.

Beryl took a step towards him, her long skirts rustling. "You weren't in Gemma's room, were you? You haven't been fiddling, have you?"

"Certainly not!" retorted Oswin indignantly. "I wanted a word with her."

"Well you can't," replied Beryl. "She's in the bathroom and needs her privacy respected at such times."

Oswin narrowed his eyes and seethed quietly for a moment. Then he balked, his eyes widening. "Actually, I think you'll find that she is not in the bathroom."

"Of course she is! I heard her slam the door," insisted Beryl. She stalked across the landing to the bathroom door and flung it open. She stood in the doorway, her hand still poised on the doorknob, and looked about. Then she turned back to Oswin, "It definitely slammed. Ah, so it was you—you said you were looking for Gemma! Try to be more gentle with the furnishings of this house please, Oswin, or someone could get hurt!"

He took a step towards her, protesting his innocence, but she cut him off by raising her hand, "No!" she said firmly, before changing her tune to sound quite coy. "I need the bathroom now. You and Gemma don't mind waiting, do you? But don't queue, I can't get my make up on evenly with someone hovering outside the door. It's the pressure, you know! I hope you don't mind!" She grinned cheerfully at him, as she shut the door.

Oswin shuddered. Oh, that Beryl! Her bossiness was bad enough, but the way she kept trying to sugarcoat it with supposed subservience was beyond annoying—it was disturbing. Oswin had seen at family gatherings, aunts and nan's—and even his own mum!—tut-tutting about 'poor Gemma's emotional problems'. But he spent proper time here and now he knew the truth. As far as Oswin was concerned, there was nothing the matter with Gemma at all. She was as well adjusted as she could be with a family like hers. If it weren't for Gemma, he'd tell Beryl and their father where to put their enormous 'Edwardian Terraced' and go to his school's hostel. And gladly put up with the rich ogre types shoving his head down the loo and sneaking punches at him for cracking a maths test. He had fellow 'gifted' friends in the hostel, so he knew what weedy boffins put up with there.

Oswin was half done packing his book bag when he remembered his unfinished cereal in the kitchen and went downstairs, just in time to see Gemma tip-toeing upstairs again.

She mouthed, "Is she still in the bathroom?" as she passed him on the stairs.

He nodded and continued on into the kitchen. The contents of his bowl were so soggy and dismal that he threw them away and poured himself out a new helping. To his annoyance, Beryl soon joined him, spreading two slices of toast with liberal helpings of marmalade, and pointedly reading a paper as she chewed noisily. Once or twice, she muttered things like, "Serves them right!" and "Oh, my Gawd!" as she slurped marmalade off her fingers and turned the page.

Oswin made no response. He stared into his cereal, out of the window, at the clock—anything rather than converse with Beryl. And then there it was again. A shadow—a movement—just out of focus, above the clock. But when he looked—nothing. Just a tingle of gooseflesh. He frowned. Nope. Surely he imagined it and he imagined it because he expected—wanted—to see it again. But he could feel eyes boring down on him. He could just feel he was being watched.

It was Beryl. She stared at Oswin from across the table, then, throwing her paper aside, she thumped her fist down. Her toast bounced on the plate.

"You are not helping!" she boomed.

The flowers in the vase quivered. Oswin, although not yet thirteen, was made of stronger stuff. He looked at her inquiringly.

"You are not supposed to go *'Ga-Ga'* on us," Beryl continued. "You were invited to board with us in order not only to assist your parents' financial burden of rearing a gifted child—as you know the cost of public schooling—but also to help *our* family situation. That is, to promote stability by helping us draw Gemma out of herself. Your mother is always going on about your common sense and genius," she embellished bitterly, "but you're making things worse!"

Beryl enjoyed spouting off long monologues. It made her feel sophisticated.

"What? I looked at the clock. What is wrong with looking at a clock?"

"It's the *way* you did it!" Beryl accused loudly. She seldom spoke quietly.

"Ah." Oswin folded his skinny arms and lent back in his chair and asked with mocking eloquence, "Would you be kind enough, my dear cousin, to demonstrate to me, preferably in slow motion, how you would like me to look up at the clock?"

The hue of her ruddy face deepened further. "You're supposed to look at it to see the time! You thought you saw something out of the corner of your eye!" She punctuated her accusation with an aggressive stare. Her eyes seemed more watery than ever.

Oswin wondered how they never melted away altogether. He blinked at her innocently.

"Do you know what I am thinking now?" he asked levelly—sweetly. "Perhaps you could tell me what I am planning to do for my next science project? Because for the love of Mike, *I* can't come up with any good ideas! None that I'm aware of," he finished irritably.

In the dining room, further along the hall, the framed Van Gough print crashed to the floor. They both ignored it. Beryl had put it up there to replace the old clock and loved referring to it as 'The Van Gough.'

Gazing down her ample cleavage at some crumbs that had become wedged there and begun to tickle, Beryl picked them out with her broad, manicured fingers, flicking them onto her plate with studied elegance.

Then she continued, "Do you know how long it's taken me to get Gemma back to some semblance of normality, after we lost Mother? And I use the term 'normality' broadly. As you know, she is under observation by the child welfare authorities. That is to say, Gemma is under constant threat of being committed to a child psychiatric unit at the nearest large hospital." Here she paused to place a hand on her bosom as a shudder rippled through her.

"And a fine job you've done too," remarked Oswin. "She's a perfectly normal twelve year old."

Beryl continued loftily, "The death of Mother has had an enormous effect on her sense of reality. Her foundation was ripped from beneath her. She was grasping at anything to fill the gap of not having a mother figure, despite everything that Father and I did for her in trying to replace what she'd lost. I don't think she'll ever be totally right, but she has calmed down a bit with regards to her strange beliefs." Beryl paused to dab her eyes with a handy tissue. She always carried things like handy tissues and combs.

Oswin rolled his eyes wearily and slurped his sweet, corn flake milk. It was best just to sit it out. There was no stopping Beryl once she got going, and it looked like this morning's spiel was going to be a long one. Beryl didn't know she was alive unless she was sloshing around in her Bog of Melodrama.

"We have already moved from our original family abode of happiness," sniffed Beryl, "in order to escape the ghostly memories of my mother. I simply had no choice but to insist we move out of that house. Mother's spirit was lingering so strongly—God-rest-her-soul—that I couldn't escape it and get on with the task of rearing Gemma, whilst keeping up with my studies. It was the most difficult decision I have had to make. And I've had to make many since being forced to step into Mother's shoes." Beryl stuffed the last of her toast into her mouth and chewed thoughtfully. Her watery eyes fixed in a morose upward stare.

A spark lit up in Oswin's busy head.

"Did Gemma *'see'* things there? Like you did?" he asked.

"No. It wasn't like Mother was *haunting* it," replied Beryl caustically, reaching for another slice of toast. "That wasn't the sort of thing she would do! She would never want to cause us any pain! It was the memories. Her presence was still there. I don't think I can explain it to you properly. You are, after all, only a pre-pubescent,"

Oswin opened his mouth but had no time to retort as Beryl continued, "And what I'm talking about involves emotional maturity, not mere intellect, which—gifted or not—you, as a pre-pubescent boy, have not yet obtained," she finished. And smiled. That was another apparently unintentional insult.

"So, although Gemma felt your mother's presence in the old house," he confirmed, "she's only been *'seeing things'* here—in this house?"

"We all most certainly did—in reality—feel the presence of Mother, God-Rest-Her-Soul, in that house. And since we moved here, I don't think Gemma has got *worse*," Beryl said, bristling. "And I am keeping an eye on her, and following her progress, as it were. I think moving here has helped to bring some closure to our bereavement, you know." She smacked her lips and gave her cousin a purposeful stare.

"Yes, but *seeing things* has only been here?" Oswin tried again.

"And after reading the report of the assessment on Gemma's mental health, by the Department of Child Psychology, I am positive that I made the right decision to move us to this house. The report said, after all, *'Gemma's behavior remains within the realms of normality,'* " Beryl quoted.

"I know, I agree with you but...."

"She was bound to have a settling-in period. Besides, they assured me that it's just a bit of an overactive imagination, that's all," Beryl declared sternly. "And if we *don't* feed it, Gemma will be perfectly well adjusted and happy."

Oswin threw his hands up and sighed. "Yes, yes I see! Beryl, you are perfectly right."

She nodded triumphantly. Ran her tongue across her teeth, and said, "And that is why I say: Don't look at the clock like that!"

He nodded.

"Because there's nothing there."

He nodded again.

"And she doesn't need to see people thinking they've *seen things* too." Beryl took another enormous bite of her toast and chewed slowly. With deliberation. Staring hard at Oswin.

He longed to point out while her mouth was full that Gemma hadn't seen him see the shadow on the stupid old clock. But he nodded instead. Politely.

Once Beryl swallowed, she laughed. Brushed imaginary crumbs off the table and said, "Sorry, Oswin! I just had to get that straight with you. We want you two to be friends, but don't encourage her in any airy-fairy stuff, please! Just snakes and ladders and other *innocent* games will do. It's very important that Gemma is not led astray. Ghosts and that sort of thing do not exist. It's a proven fact." She smiled again.

Oswin bit his tongue so hard he could have sliced it off. He put a great deal of energy into scraping his empty bowl.

"Snakes and ladders!" he mouthed with a sneer. Then once more, he froze. As he slowly looked up at Beryl, a smile spread over his face.

"You're not angry with me, are you?" Beryl asked. She cocked her head to one side. "I know you are a highly intelligent boy, and mature for your age, but I am five and a quarter years your senior, and thus more experienced in life than you. And I do hold the *adult* position of lady of the house."

Oswin shook his head vaguely.

"I mean," continued Beryl, getting knotted up, "if I seem older than my years, it's because I am. I had to grow up suddenly to become mother to my sister, who was only six at the time. And for a girl of almost twelve years—as I was then, which you can work out with your excellent mathematics skills—taking up the position of lady of the house is an enormous task. Luckily, I was already mature beyond my yea..." Beryl broke off, aware at last that Oswin was not listening. "What is it? I'm very intuitive, you know, and I sense something's wrong." She leaned forward and put one hand gently onto her chest.

"No, no, my dear cousin," Oswin replied absently, his mind whirring away merrily. "Nothing's wrong at all. In fact," he stood up, grappling with his jacket, "I've just had a wicked idea. That project—I know what I'm going to do it on!"

"What project? What are you on about?" Beryl called after him. But he had walked away. She swiped more crumbs off the table, thinking, *Boffins! They always have to put on this mad professor act!*

Oswin, meanwhile, bumped into Gemma just as she came tripping down the stairs, her eyes wide and darting as she approached the dim hall.

"Alright, Gem! Haven't you left for school yet?" Oswin said with a broad grin. He punched the air, making a little jump as he did.

Gemma grinned back at him. "What's all that about?"

"I have just decided what I'm going to do that project on," he declared, all teeth still.

Gemma's hand fluttered about her mouth, as though she longed to bite her nails, but dared not. "Oh, good! What's it going to be?"

Looking round to check that Beryl was not within earshot, Oswin leaned forwards to whisper in Gemma's ear.

Her eyebrows arched and then she glanced about to ensure they *were* quite alone. "Really?" she gasped. Her hand settled for a moment over her mouth, and she giggled.

Oswin's face scowled determinedly. "So help me God!" he growled between clenched teeth.

Chapter Two

Gemma crept into the kitchen-diner and began to clear the table. Her movements were careful. Quiet.

"Haven't you left for school yet?" Beryl asked, coming up behind her.

She jumped and squeaked. "It's my turn to do the breakfast dishes."

Gemma hoped Beryl would rush upstairs now, brush her teeth or something, but she didn't. She hovered, asking annoying questions.

"Did you have any nightmares?"

"No," Gemma said, and thought to herself, *Sorry to disappoint, but I had a wonderful dream, actually.*

"Are you alright? No tummy aches?"

"No. I'm fine!"

"Are you sure? You can tell me," Beryl prodded further.

Gemma didn't reply to this; humming the theme song from *Shrek*, she put the milk back in the fridge. Beryl stared at her and sighed, waiting.

"Well, have you seen the ghost again?" she asked flatly.

Gemma regarded her with wide, brown eyes and began to stack the crockery into the dishwasher with more clatter than was necessary.

"No." Thanks to Beryl's fussing, this whole ghost thing had been blown out of proportion.

"I know Father said to not mention ghosts ever," Beryl said, eyeing her tentatively, "but you can tell me about anything. I know how real this is for you. And it must be frightening each time you *think* you see it. I remember how upset I would get in the old house when I was reminded of Mother." She waited for a reply, but got none. Gemma still had her back to her, sorting the cutlery. Busy.

After a while, she gave Gemma's shoulders a little squeeze. "Call me if you see anything. Anything strange at all."

Gemma stopped her task for a moment and turned to face her. "Okay, Beryl, I will. Next time I see a ghost I'll come and call you." Perhaps that was the only way she'd get Beryl to see what she was talking about.

"Honest, just call me," repeated Beryl. "But remember it's just all in your head. I'm not saying you *may* believe what you see—or that *I* believe it. But I will be there to support you."

"Yeah, alright!" Gemma's voice jarred like a knotted wind chime.

"Now, are you quite sure you're up to school?"

Gemma shut the dishwasher door with a pert click. "Yes. Quite sure."

"I can write you a note. The teachers understand about your home life being difficult. What without a mother..."

"I want to go."

Beryl smacked her lips, as though contemplating a tasty morsel. "Well, shall I write you a note to explain why you're late? Because I'm sure you're going to be late."

"I'm not. I won't be."

But Beryl was already rummaging around in the dresser for pen and paper.

Gemma sighed, went to get her school things, leaving Beryl to amuse herself with writing a note and complaining about being delayed herself.

"I'll have to write a note for me too at this rate!" Beryl laughed nervously, before giving in to mild hysteria. "This is making me late. How do you spell Mister Smith—is it '*i-t-h*' or '*y-t-h-e*'? Oh, me gawd! I haven't had time to brush my teeth yet! Gemma, come back here a minute!"

Gemma stood wordlessly in the doorway, putting her blazer on.

"Ah, there you are!" said Beryl, breathlessly. "The Van Gough fell down again earlier on. Hang it back up, there's a good girl! I haven't the time. I've been busy sorting your school note." She handed it to Gemma.

"Me? The Van Gough?" stammered Gemma, taking the note and shoving it absently in her pockets. "I can't. I'm too frightened."

"Don't be silly. It's only a print," insisted Beryl, adjusting Gemma's collar. "Quickly now, I'm late."

Gemma sighed, squared her shoulders and ran through to the dining room chanting a tuneless stream of, "la la la la la la..."

She thought the dining room was a truly horrid room. It was dark and cold, as it never got direct sunlight streaming in. But what really troubled Gemma about the dining room was that she always felt as though someone was in there. Staring at her. Her heart pounded, the feeling of being watched intensified. "La la la la...where is it?...la la la la..." Spotting the picture, she snatched it up. It had a crack in the glass, but she ignored that. She struggled, standing on tip-toes, to fix it onto its hook, fancied she heard a whispering behind her and tried to ignore that too. Her movements became more frantic as she cringed, waiting for that touch, that tap on the shoulder. Gemma let out a sob—the darn loop wouldn't grip onto the hook—one last try, then giving up, she dumped the Van Gough on the table and fled the room. The door slammed behind her with a *bang!* Gemma jumped clean into the air as she ran. Her ballet teacher would have been proud.

"La la la la..." She bolted passed Beryl and up the stairs.

"Honest, Gemma; don't slam the doors!"

But she didn't hear. Her fingers were still in her ears. "...la la la la..."

After doing a series of ballet positions, she managed to calm herself enough to gather her school bag up and leave the house for the sanctuary of the school halls.

* * * *

By that evening, Oswin's research was well under way. He staggered in, pushing the door open with his shoulder, his keys in his mouth, and a mound of library books in his arms. He disappeared to his room, emerging only when Beryl rang her dinner bell. Yes, she actually had a dinner bell and used it to summon the two younger ones to the table.

After they had eaten their meal, he hurried back to his room and had already filled in at least a quarter of a standard refill pad with his own notes when Gemma joined him. She brought them a mug of coffee each, setting Oswin's down beside him where he sat at his desk, pouring over his books, and perched herself on the foot of his bed. She'd left his door open, as was the rule. Her father, Griswold, insisted if any of the girls were alone in a room with Oswin, for whatever purpose and for no matter how long, the door was to remain wide open. Gemma felt embarrassed—indignant—at Griswold's Victorian distrust. But she complied with the rule. Oswin shrugged off his uncle's paranoia and concentrated on the important things. Like his homework and projects.

"Did you know," he asked now, "that ghosts actually caught on camera have been few and far between; undisputed recordings, that is?" He removed his specs and rubbed them clean with a tissue.

"Well, that doesn't seem very helpful," Gemma sighed and curled her fingers round her mug, hunching over it. "How are you going to prove that ghosts existence, then?"

"I've changed the study to general paranormal activity. And I'll have a far greater chance of recording fluctuations in the temperature and magnetic fields in the house." Oswin replaced his glasses, rubbed his left ear and continued. "Ghost hunters seem to explain away most hauntings as central heating pipes playing up and old floorboards contracting as the temperature drops." Those were also Griswold's and Beryl's answers.

"Who's side are they on?"

"No, they've got a point," Oswin said. "All these theories have to be disproved before one can announce a real, actual haunting. Ghosts are obviously some sort of energy field," he continued, eyes sparkling. "Just part of a whole spectrum of paranormal activity. In fact, there are different types of ghosts too. But often there's a logical explanation for many hauntings."

Gemma muttered a vague agreement, and stared absently into the landing.

"But don't worry, Gem, even if I have to title my work, 'Do Ghosts Exist?' or 'A Study of the Difficulties of Recording Paranormal Activity,' I'll prove to that big bummed, wind-bag Beryl that you've been right all along! And to Griswold! We'll show them just exactly *who* is a bit funny, eh?"

Gemma forced her gaze back towards her cousin and smiled briefly. She sipped her coffee, gently blowing the steam into swirling billows, while Oswin pottered about.

After a pause he continued, "And I've already started building a device to take the readings with."

He turned from his work and grinned at her, arched his eyebrows wickedly. Rubbed his hands together, "The first prototype!"

Gemma grinned back nervously. "*X-Files* step aside!"

Oswin's laughter wasn't exactly diabolical, but it darn near hit the spot; she quickly finished her coffee, and stood up.

"Well, I'll let you get on."

"Right-O!" Oswin shuffled comfortably and bent over his books again. "Oh, by the way," he said, lifting his head momentarily, "once I've taken an initial reading of the house, call me straight away if you see the ghost, yeah?"

* * * *

In the next few days Oswin finished building his meters and Gemma flitted about the house, between school and dance lessons. She felt relaxed enough to enjoy watching telly, even if it meant sitting in the front room—another part of the house that unnerved her. Her Dad forbid them to have a telly in their rooms.

She stopped by in Oswin's room one evening to confide in him. "Things actually seem calmer," she said. "Like, I don't feel so creepy. Perhaps it was my imagination. Perhaps it's all gone away?" She gazed apologetically at Oswin's desk. It was cluttered with tools, wires and little boards. Strange boards, decked with silver roads, tiny drums and flat roofed buildings. "It looks like a miniature city," she said, picking one of them up and studying it, turning it this way and that.

Oswin guffawed and shook his head, smiling to himself. "But as for the lull in paranormal activities, don't worry, Gem. That's just the way it is with these things. Ghosts are notorious for not performing on demand!" He gave her a knowing look and cracked his knuckles, bent over his work again. "You just get on with your normal routine. Keep busy. They'll soon come out of hiding."

So, she watched her favorite DVDs, the *Shrek* films, over and over. And she began to develop a serious crush on the green ogre. In fact, when Rebecca Wilson from school told Gemma she would be invited to her fancy dress disco party at the end of term, she knew exactly who she'd be going as. If Griswold allowed her to go, of course.

On Saturday, having got back from Miss Jemima Maple's Academy of Dance, and realizing she could have the front room to herself, Gemma decided to watch *Shrek* yet again. Griswold—who would normally watch the football there—was still at work and Beryl was shut away, studying and unlikely to bother her.

Gemma hummed the theme tune as she made coffee and fetched the biscuit tin down, happily practising a basic ballet position whilst balancing the DVD in its case on the tin on one hand and holding her coffee with the other. All without spilling or dropping anything. Satisfied, she smiled as she carried the lot through the shadowy hall into the living room, the tune still skipping in her mind.

"Ta-da-dee. Ta-da-da. Ta-da-de..." Her humming broke off abruptly, mutating into a short, stifled scream as she stopped dead, almost dropping the tin, and letting the DVD slide off and bump onto the carpet.

The ghost sat in Griswold's chair, facing the telly, knitting with a dowdy brown yarn. Her movements were rhythmic, monotonous, like the ticking of a clock and she looked quite solid, not at all see through. Her hair was tied up with a scarf, knotted on the top, keeping her curlers in place. Over her dowdy cotton dress, she wore a faded housecoat. Her face was as drab and unemotional as her clothing. Even when she turned—without pausing in her knitting—to stare demurely at Gemma, she betrayed no emotion apart from a hint of sourness. The ghost emanated that desolate emotion—and it rippled out from her, filling the room, seeping into Gemma's own emotions, and mingling negatively with the wave of fear and shock that drenched her.

Gemma uttered a stifled scream, backing out of the room hastily. "It...it...the... Aaah!" She floundered senselessly in the hall, running on the spot in tight little jogs, convinced the housewife ghost was coming up behind her. She dashed into the kitchen, dripping a trail of coffee all the way. She dumped the biscuits and DVD on the counter, circled the room a couple of times, then shoved the mug onto the table and made a frenzied dash for the stairs, flapping her hands, as though she'd burnt herself.

"Oswin! *Oswin!*" she squealed, taking the stairs in twos. Regaining her balance on the landing, she remembered he was out. He had gone on a hunt for maps of Ley-lines. At least he'd be back later that day. Gemma thanked heavens he had not been able to go home for the weekend.

She leaned against the wall, taking several deep breaths, and eyeing the staircase nervously. She pressed her hand against her chest, murmured re-assuring words to herself. "Right...Okay...It's all gone..."

She did another series of ballet positions. Untidy, clumsy efforts, but the routine soothed her. She began to feel calmer. She stared at Beryl's bedroom door hesitantly. After a moment she gave a slight shrug and edged across the landing and knocked on Beryl's door timidly. Beryl had shut herself up in her room to do revision, declaring that she was under no circumstances to be disturbed, and Gemma kind of hoped it would not be answered. But it was.

"Come!" Beryl called from within, and Gemma opened the door.

A four poster bed, large and ornate, enveloped in a frothy quilt and voluptuous pillows, took up most of the spacious room. A heavy, wooden dressing table was engulfed in a clutter of lotions and potions. Silk scarves and bead necklaces cascaded down the wing mirrors. There was a desk, squashed into a corner between the built in cupboard and the window. But it was no use as a desk. It was piled up with books and stationary. Beryl sat on the fluffy carpeted floor, like an Eastern empress, encircled by a scattering of textbooks, files and loose paper. Staring at some scrawled notes as she absently chewed on a Paper Mate pen, she did not acknowledge Gemma's entrance.

Gemma, white-faced, frailer than ever, reeled in the doorway, and squeaked brokenly, "B...Beryl, I saw it! The...it's..."

Beryl looked up, indicating with her outstretched hand. "Mind the papers!"

Gemma tiptoed into the room, hovering uncertainly in an effort to find a path through Beryl's studying.

"Downstairs! Nnngggh!" she spluttered, almost losing her balance.

"Don't stand on that book! It's irreplaceable!"

Gemma froze as she stood, one foot in mid-air, arms stretched out in order to balance herself, making full use of years of ballet lessons. She swallowed hard, and muttered, "Sorry!" Then taking a deep breath, she continued more calmly, "Okay. I've just seen it."

"What?" asked Beryl, a look of hopefulness washing over her face. "You've found my Coast sweater?"

Gemma frowned, finding enough space for both feet on the floor and repositioning herself slightly. "No. The ghost! It's in the front room! Downstairs—I've just seen her."

Beryl stared for a moment then blinking, replied, "I wonder where my sweater's got to?"

"*The ghost!*" Gemma hissed urgently, arms flapping, fists clenched. "It's sitting there now, come and see!"

"All right, all right, I know—your ghost! And don't stand on that one either, it's on loan from the library! I'm coming!" Beryl rolled her eyes, rose awkwardly to her feet and treading through the mess as she spoke, stepping heavily on the library book herself, without realizing it

"Now, show me this ghost of yours!" she said, grasping Gemma by the shoulders and steering her out onto the landing.

Chapter Three

Gemma wriggled free and skittered down the stairs, slowing nervously as they reached the last few steps. She allowed Beryl to cling, giggling, to her arm as they crept into the living room.

It was quite lifeless. As she stared into it, Gemma realized what a gloomy looking room it was, even without the ghost. It was furnished in a drab lounge suite of heavy fabrics, earthy colors. Although the window was fairly wide, it got no direct sunlight, was dim most of the time, and now was no exception.

"There now, you see!" snorted Beryl victoriously. "I keep telling you, it's that overactive imagination of yours." She strode into the room, did a couple of pirouettes as she spoke and stopped to smile triumphantly at Gemma.

Gemma bit her lip, and said quietly yet determinedly. "No. It was there! Sitting in Dad's chair. You would have seen her too…"

"Aha! 'In *Father's* chair!' Don't you see?" Beryl paused, with that maddening grin plastered on her face, waiting to see if Gemma would catch on to the psychological conclusion, but she stared back with a poker face, trying to hide her raging irritation at her older sister's condescending smugness.

Beryl puffed up and concluded in a professional voice, "The fact that the illusion occurred in Father's chair, at a time when *he* should have been in it, indicates that you were obviously wishing he were home. Don't you see? You poor little thing!" she crooned sympathetically, stepping forward to lay a caring hand on Gemma's burning cheek.

Gemma stiffened, staring fixedly at the wall speckled with school photos still in cardboard studio frames. "Fine! Whatever!"

Beryl guided her out of the room into the hallway. "Let's go and have a cup of tea!"

She put the kettle on quickly and efficiently, talking all the time with grating kindness. "It's your nervous disposition. It's a pity you're too young for something like Calmets. Holland and Barrett do loads of herbal stuff too. Perhaps we could just go and find something there without trying to bleed a prescription out of these NHS doctors."

Gemma stood with folded arms and said nothing.

Beryl's monologue was interrupted, however, when she slipped in some of Gemma's coffee spill.

Flailing her arms, she managed to stay upright. "Oh, me gawd! What was that? There's something on the floor!"

She bent down and peered, frowning at the floor, reached out and tentatively wiped her forefinger across the offending area.

Gemma watched her. "Actually, that was me. I must have spilt some coffee when..."

"Well, surely you know enough to wipe it up!"

"Sorry!" Gemma rushed over to the sink to fetch a rag. "Sorry, but..."

"No, that won't be enough! You'll need a cleaner to spray on it first. It looks like it's setting on the floor already," Beryl cut in, still bent over the coffee spill, and examining it as though it were a fungus from the moon.

Gemma sighed and began rummaging in the cupboard under the taps.

After watching her young sister for a moment, Beryl said, "Why don't you make us a cup of tea, now that we're here? You always make a good cuppa. Besides, I've got to get back to my work. Two of our lecturers gave us homework, plus we've got two tests. *Two!* And you know how close the exams are. I don't know how I'm going to have it all done by Monday, honest to goodness I don't. It's so unfair! This form six college is so *hard*. Why did they have to change the system, just as I was getting there? Just wait until Oswin gets to that level then we'll see how brilliant he really is. I'm sure he doesn't get pushed this hard in his hoity-toity *public...*" and her voice trailed off as she disappeared upstairs.

But it started up again, like a neighbor's lawn mower on a Sunday morning, as she hung over the banister, driving her point home. "Just bring my tea up when it's made, okay? Sorry, but I really can't come down and sit with you! I know you've had a fright and all that, but I can't spare the time. I just don't know how I'm supposed to cope. All the other kids only have their exams to worry about, but I've got all these other responsibilities as well!"

Gemma heard her saying how unfair life was, as she shut her bedroom door.

"Well, I'll try not to be too much bother," she muttered and dropped to her hands and knees and rubbed the floor vigorously.

Beryl's overly gracious thanks, when Gemma brought her a cup of tea, irritated her even more. She stalked back into the kitchen, her face twisted with anger as she mouthed Beryl's words, *'Thank you, Darling. Ooh! that's lovely. You really make the best tea, ever!'* She thumped about, pushing the kitchen chairs roughly into their positions around the table. She didn't feel like having any tea herself and shoved her cup aside and stared, brooding, at the *Shrek* DVD. Why couldn't he be real? He'd soon put Beryl right. Life with Shrek would be heavenly!

Would Shrek even fancy her—provided Princess Fiona was out of the picture—would he go for her? None of the boys in school seemed to fancy her. They didn't seem to even see her. She was far too ugly to turn heads at school.

Not that that would bother Shrek, in fact it would be an advantage. Although, she was a bit skinny for his taste. But then, a couple of years living off doughnuts and custard creams would put that right! And the odd pimple that she'd get from such enjoyable binging wouldn't be a problem. He'd prefer her to be spotty.

Yes, indeed, Shrek was the perfect bloke, a girl could really let herself go and he'd just love her even more! Although, she wasn't the right color for a ogre's bride. He'd like her to be green.

"And I'm not," she sighed mournfully. "Oh, if only I were big boned and green!"

Absently, she knelt down where the coffee had spilt and, forgetting that she'd already cleaned it, she squirted more cleaning liquid onto the floor, and began mopping it all over again, thinking how much better life would be if only she were overweight and green. Then she got to pondering, as she sprayed the floor some more, how she was going to look green for Rebecca Wilson's party, which was a far more realistic issue at hand. A green Princess Fiona would be instantly recognizable, but dressed as the normal, daytime Princess Fiona, Gemma would look like any another medieval lady. Not even her perfectly colored red hair would give any clues to the other kids. They had probably forgotten the *Shrek* films. They'd end up snorting with laughter in her face. Or, worse still, giggling maliciously behind her back. No, her red hair was not going to be enough to pull it off—she had to go green for the party. But how?

"Of course!" she cried out. "Yes, I know!"

Chapter Four

Why hadn't she thought of it before?

"Yes! Why not?"

Rising up, forgetting the spray bottle and the new, wet patch on the floor, Gemma declared out loud, "I *can* actually go green!"

Actors dyed their hair for certain roles and skin could be dyed too. Temporarily, of course, but it could be done. Just for fun. And it wouldn't be dyed as such, merely painted. If she had enough money, that is. In order to get it just right for the party, she decided to try it out at home first, right there and then. That very day.

Gemma danced upstairs to fetch her purse. Hoping rather than checking that she had enough money, she skipped back down, and was just reaching out to open the door when Oswin opened it from outside, almost crashing into her.

"Oh, hello, Oswin!" she greeted him breathlessly. "I'm just going out!"

"Alright Gem?" he smiled wearily, shutting the door. "Well, when you get back in, I've got something really important to show you."

"Okay!" She hung back. "Oh, by the way, I saw the ghost today."

Oswin spun round to face her again, his eyes aglow. "When? Where? Why didn't you say so?"

"In the sitting room," Gemma flinched. "Er...about half an hour ago, I think. Maybe more." She twirled a wisp of hair around her fingers.

"Why didn't you say?"

"I did. Just now—as you came in."

"Right." Oswin paced the tiny hall. "Yes, of course. Oh, Gemma, you'll have to be more specific! I've got to have proper recordings to see if my ghost detector works. Here, hold this!" He dumped a pile of papers in her arms and raced up the stairs, two at a time, calling, "This is more than just another project!"

Gemma stared after him. Half of the papers slipped out of her arms and cascaded down to the floor. Hurriedly, she gathered them all together. There seemed to be some maps mixed in with some photocopies. She found them a space on the Welsh dresser.

"Oswin, I'm sorry," she said as he bounded down the stairs

towards her. "They're mixed up now!"

He made no reply—only grinned proudly as he showed her what he had run up to fetch. He was brandishing a gadget which looked like a hair straightener with lines of LEDs where the plastic bristles should be, down the sides of the cylinder. Two short aerials protruded out of the tip. The handle was large and flat, to allow for a few buttons and dials, and an impressive little display unit.

"Wow!" breathed Gemma, turning it round and gazing at it. "What is it?"

"This little gadget," Oswin crooned, "measures the magnetism in the atmosphere, picking up the magnetic fields..."

"But what are the fairy lights for?"

"LEDs. They're a visual indicator of the velocity of..." He broke off, realizing that Gemma was glazing over. "They light up when a ghost is detected. And the antennas draw together, like a divining rod. Plus I've put in an audio indicator as well—that is, it makes a clicking sound too!"

Gemma nodded, her eyes widening.

"In this note book," Oswin continued, passing her an exercise book, which she immediately pledged to cover in pretty paper for him, "I've recorded the readings I took yesterday and the day before. Now is the chance to see if the ghost's appearance has altered the magnetic fields in the area!"

"Oswin, you're brilliant!"

He blushed and ran his fingers through his hair. "So, take me to your ghost!"

Gemma tiptoed through to the living room and showed him exactly where and how the ghost had sat.

"In Griswold's own chair?" he tut-tutted. "What a cheek!"

Gemma giggled then fell silent, as she became aware of Oswin's intense concentration.

He 'ah!-ed' and frowned, and 'um-ed' as the ghost detector clicked softly, flashing its LEDs briefly before falling silent. The antenna didn't move. Oswin handed her a pen and read out the results, and she printed them neatly in the book, comparing the new readings to the first ones. Her eyebrows arched briefly.

"They're a *bit* higher," she observed cautiously. She looked to Oswin for confirmation and he peered at the notebook.

"Mm, it does indicate a slight disturbance," he said after a moment's reflection, "but not anything to get excited over. Plus," here he peered out of the window, "Plus, it looks like rain —a static build-up in the air, you know, may be a factor."

"Mm." Gemma bit the top of the pen and stared sadly at the figures on the page, willing them to be what Oswin wanted, absently pointing her toes, one foot at a time; in, out...in, out. Her cousin scratched his head.

"Do you know," he said at last, brightening up, "I think we should take the weather into account—always. Put a column in to note the weather conditions at the time of the readings!"

"Brilliant!" she squeaked.

"Excuse me!" demanded Beryl, from the doorway. "But what are you two up to?"

They whipped round, like infants caught with their hands in the cookie jar. Gemma glanced at Oswin, looking for a cue.

He decided to come clean, and clearing his throat, he replied loftily, "Nothing. Just taking readings—to see if there are traces of...er...paranormal activity...or, in other words, the ghost," he finished somewhat indistinctly.

"I know the meaning of paranormal activity, thank you," replied Beryl frostily and loudly. "But there's nothing there."

"Ahem...precisely! So you've nothing to worry about!" Oswin clutched at Gemma's bony arm, leaning close to her to whisper a quick message. "I should get there straight away next time. Call me on my mobile, no matter where or when, yeah?"

She nodded in reply, holding the note book close to her chest, and stared hard at a place just left of Beryl's knees.

"What are you whispering about? And what's that *thing* you're holding, Oswin?" Beryl accused, taking her turn at haughtiness and managing it admirably. She eyed him suspiciously.

"We're just trying out my ghost detector. I invented it. Yes, my dear cousin, that's right. I said, *'Ghost Detector!'*"

"I've really got to go," Gemma gushed frantically, sensing a bit of a Waterloo. "I was just on my way out, remember?"

Oswin glanced at her, "Right. Remember, call any time!"

"What *is* that thing?" Beryl repeated, advancing towards him, as Gemma slipped out of the room. "It's not some sort of Vidal Sassoon gadget, is it?"

Oswin glared up at her through his specs. "No! I'm highly patriotic and espionage is not my cup of tea! I've just told you, I made it myself—for the ghost!"

"I know, I heard you!" Beryl snapped. She continued to close in on him, a hand outstretched. "It looks suspiciously like my missing hair straighteners to me—let me see that!"

He dodged her. "It's nothing of the sort! It's a device to detect the possible presence..."

"Then why won't you give it to me?" Beryl strained to reach it.

"You'd break it!" Oswin cried, jumping over the coffee table and making for the door. But Beryl pursued him relentlessly.

Whilst their chase began in the living room, Gemma—at that very moment—bumped into Griswold just outside the front door.

"Oh! Um...hello, Dad! Bye, Dad, I'll be back soon!"

"Hello," he replied, red-faced in his effort to get to the telly in time for the game. He was a squat, balding man who wore a grey Celtic moustache. It made him look permanently grumpy. "What are you looking so guilty about? Hey?" he asked.

"I'm trying to get to town before everything shuts," Gemma fretted. "Um...Dad, would the stagecraft shop sell body paint? Or should I try the crafts and hobbies shop?"

"Both, I should think," he advised, frowning. "Now don't be out long—be home for tea, you hear?"

"Okay, Dad. Bye!" she called as she darted off down the road. "I've got to catch the bus!"

He watched her go and shook his head, "Darn crazy at that age they are," he muttered as he went indoors. Hearing excited voices in the kitchen, he peeled off his jacket and ambled wearily through.

Beryl, meanwhile, had Oswin pinned to the fridge, but he still held the ghost detector out of her reach.

"This is a genuine scientific project!" he declared with all the command he could muster. "If this device comes within the vicinity of a ghost it *will*..." But he had let his guard down and Beryl snatched the ghost detector with a triumphant cry.

Oswin let out a loud, high pitched yell and made a grab for the ghost detector as Beryl thundered off with remarkable speed and grace. But Oswin was quick and lithe and had her in an instant— just as she did a banana slip on Gemma's still-wet patch on the floor.

As they hurtled to the floor, with Beryl landing heavily on poor Oswin, and as Griswold opened the kitchen door onto the scene of the affray, a dark, shapeless mass bounded from behind the clock. It streaked across the room in mid-air and vanished behind the fridge. This was enough to set Oswin's device off. It shuddered into life in Beryl's hand, its antennas flailing, as it rattled off a fire of clicks, like a rattlesnake magnified, as the LEDs flashed wildly. And Beryl roared rather than screamed.

Oswin cried out hoarsely with the effort of prying the device from her hands, as though he were in great pain. He snatched the ghost detector from her and rolled up to a sitting position just as the display finished. His eyes were wide and focused and his breathing hard, as he stared in wonder at the magnificence of his creation in full action.

"Did you see that?" he hiccuped, the chase—the battle-fury— all forgotten.

Beryl, convinced she'd broken something in the struggle, groaned, and rocked on the floor.

"Yes," growled Griswold, from the doorway. The cleaning spray bottle lay leaking at his feet. His face was puce, his knuckles white and his moustache bristled. "Beryl, What are you doing attacking him with cattle prongs? We are not allowed to lay a hand on them kids nowadays! If there's any bruising on the boy, his mother—the W*elfare*—will be onto me in a shot! I know it's a disgrace the way youngsters carry on nowadays, but our hands are tied! You'll be sent away by the Welfare, and how will I cope then? With no one to look after the little ones?"

His face drained to grey as he slid into a chair, his breathing shallow.

Oswin, unable to draw his attention from his device, and unaware that he had been categorized as a 'little one,' waved Griswold's concerns aside. "These readings. Something's happened! This is great! Did you see anything, Beryl?"

Beryl, took a moment then hobbled towards Griswold. "It's not how it looks, we were fighting...Aaah!" She cried out, leaving her sentence unfinished, as she slipped again in Gemma's wet patch and landed once more in an undignified heap.

"Owwee! The bleedin' floor's wet!" However, she knew this was no time to worry about her injuries. Griswold was still staring ahead with a dangerous look in his eye, "But Father," she continued quickly, lying on the floor like a Roman lounging on a divan, "I was not punishing him. I was treating him as an equal. We were fighting over what to watch on telly. I wanted to catch *the game*, and Oswin wanted to see that stupid nature program." She paused hopefully, to see if Father had picked up her emphasis on 'the game' and taken the bait. Oswin, remembering that he was outnumbered by non-believers, as it were, slid the detector behind his back. Griswold had the power to confiscate his Ghost Detector indefinitely.

After a tense moment, Griswold blinked. "The game," he

repeated expressionlessly.

"And we were fighting over the *remote*, when we slipped on this wet floor," Beryl continued, then turned to her cousin accusingly. "Oswin, did you wet the floor?"

"No!" he frowned. Beryl obviously was under the illusion that she could be blamed for taking a part in making the device. Ha! With her flea brain? Not likely! Yet he was amazed at how fast and calculating she could be when scheming.

"You kids can't go horsing around the house like that, you're far too big!" said Griswold, returning safely to what was normal behavior for him: scolding and complaining. A lot. "Someone could have got hurt! If the authorities notice so much as a tiny mark on a kid nowadays, they put them on the At Risk List! We have to *reason* with them nowadays. No clip around the ear, or the authorities chuck the parents into jail and the kids go straight into care!"

"Excuse me! Someone *did* get hurt!" Beryl wailed indignantly, rubbing her rump and leaning on the table dramatically as she clamored up to her feet.

"You're right, Griswold, I'm so sorry! Don't know what came over me," muttered Oswin. Then he said with deliberate clarity, "I'll just put the *remote* next to the *telly*!" He slipped out of the kitchen before Beryl could stop him, making a graceful beeline for his room. He had plenty of notes to scribble out, and once Griswold got started about At Risk lists, he could go on for ages.

"No! Put the telly on for the match!" Griswold said pointedly to Oswin's hastily retreating back then he turned to Beryl. "Make us a pot of tea, Luv. That was a dreadful fright you gave me...I thought for a moment you were torturing the boy...ugh!" He shuddered.

Chapter Five

Later that day Oswin worked at his next construction, illicitly using a welding iron to make some sort of helmet with an intricate array of electronics worked into it. Brazenly flaunting Griswold's rule forbidding welding, sawing and drilling in the house, Oswin left his door wide open as he worked. He didn't want to miss Gemma's return. When she came back, he called her and she hung in the doorway, holding a small paper bag with her purchases, and listened to his account of what had happened in the kitchen earlier.

"Didn't you see anything, when the detector went off?" she asked.

"No. I was so involved in wrestling with Beryl that I wouldn't have noticed a freight train going passed my nose," Oswin replied regretfully, "And the lack of any actual sighting at the time makes the readings seem dodgy." He sighed and switched his forbidden soldering iron off at the wall. "I just hope she hadn't broken the thing and set it off."

"Well, it seems to be working excellently. Also, if the readings were slightly high in the living room ages after I saw my ghost, then wouldn't the kitchen still show a slightly higher than normal reading shortly after it went off, like that?"

He nodded and rummaged about for a piece of paper. "Yes, and it has. But as none of us actually saw anything it...Ah, here it is!" He handed Gemma the page of recordings. "Will you copy this down into the diary I gave you? I've taken readings on ten-minute intervals, and they have been coming back down. They're almost normal now."

"That's brilliant!" Gemma grinned. "Isn't it?"

Oswin adjusted his specs and agreed. "But I think we need to do recordings around quite a few sightings before we've got something concrete. I need to be very thorough with researching this project. It's a tricky subject."

"You would have been ultra-thorough anyway—you always are!" Gemma said and did a celebratory double twirl.

"I suppose so. And I'm improving the ghost detector system with this visor I'm making. I'm hoping to be able to see the ghost's aura—which is made of magnetic fields."

"Do you think it can be done?"

"Why not? The hand device works—or seems to at any rate—and this is just an extension of the whole idea. It's the head sensor!"

Oswin proudly tried on the elaborate helmet. Gemma hung onto the jar of the door and giggled.

"You look like an android in a Sci Fi serial," she said.

Gazing through the visor, everything was dark and murky—like swimming in a peaty loch. Oswin could vaguely make out Gemma as a lighter haze, against an indistinct world of shadows.

"By the way," he said, taking off the helmet and his glasses, and rubbing his eyes, "I've discovered something interesting in the library—about your house!"

The bag rustled as Gemma absently tweaked it with her slender fingers. "Oh, what?

"This house is situated on a ley line."

Gemma stared at him for a moment. "Sorry—I haven't the slightest idea what a ley line is!"

"It's a line joining two prominent points of a landscape, usually along prehistoric tracks. But in the world of the paranormal, they also seem to join up recorded ghost sightings," explained Oswin. "Places of heightened paranormal activity are often on these lines. Weird, yeah? They often coincide with underwater streams, which is stranger still. What could water have that attracts ghosts? Or makes us see them, you might ask? Well, for one thing, water's a good conductor, you know."

By now Gemma had glazed over a bit, but Oswin was in full swing, and he went on to explain his thesis exploring the significance of magnetic fields in ghostly activity. This took a chunk out of Gemma's evening, and, thanks to Beryl hogging the bathroom, it wasn't until the next day that she had a chance to try out her nice green body paint.

* * * *

The next morning—Sunday—saw Beryl hunched over her work, which carpeted her bedroom floor again. There was an air of franticness about her studying. She had lost an afternoon watching the game with Griswold. Later, in an effort to come to terms with her ordeal of being chased down by Oswin and slipping on the floor—about which no one had shown the tiniest bit of concern!—she had spent the evening shut in the bathroom, giving herself a makeover. Next, she had to gone bed in a fancy night-gown, with a cup of cocoa, a box of chocolates and The Sound of Dolphins on her CD player.

Beryl had certainly gone to bed feeling pampered and comforted, but the next morning had woken up to a pile of unfinished work. Her misery crawled straight onto her back again as she began her revision.

Gemma, meanwhile, with a mind to test the waters, locked herself in the bathroom and emerged within the hour painted bright green and wearing the closest thing she could find to a medieval dress. Her beautiful red hair looked very striking next to her new, leafy hue. She swept it back into a plait and took it as a good omen when she saw in the mirror that it was very close in color and texture to that of Princess Fiona's.

Gemma reckoned she would be instantly recognizable as the ogre princess at the party. She was sure her classmates would be impressed with such a good costume. But just to confirm, she thought she might as well walk around as Princess Fiona at home to see what the family's reaction would be. They may even tolerate her pottering around the house dressed up as the ogre princess on the odd occasion.

Impatient to test the family's reaction, Gemma looked for someone to try it out on. Oswin had worked on his visor late into the night and seemed to be fast asleep. Griswold never left his room before midday on a Sunday, so that left Beryl. Of everyone's reactions, Gemma was least keen on getting Beryl's but her impatience to show off her striking resemblance to Princess Fiona gnawed at her. After pacing her own room restlessly, Gemma at last tapped timidly on Beryl's door.

"Come!" Beryl grunted from within.

Gemma pushed the door open slowly and emerged from the landing.

"Well, what do you think of my new look?" she asked quietly.

As they gazed at one another, Beryl was vaguely aware of how unsettled she was by the vivid contrast between Gemma's green skin and her red hair.

Gemma's hands fluttered about her face and she blinked. The green paint was irritating her eyes.

Beryl blinked too but for a different reason.

"Would you please not go *Ga Ga* on me at this time!" she bellowed at last, making poor Gemma twitch. "I've got not one, but two—yes *two* wretched, great tests to study for next week. And if that's not enough, I've got homework from all my other slave-driving teachers! It never bloody ends! Father wants me to look into getting the washing machine replaced—when I'm not keeping him company while he watches his blasted football matches! I just don't have time for more appointments with health visitors and psychological assessments. So, if it's not too much to ask, *could you please wait until after this term to freak out!*"

Beryl panted a little after this volley, and glared at her leafy hued sister.

Gemma glared back at her for a moment, before turning on her heel and departing in a swirl of green.

Her pace slackened as she trod down the stairs, unaware that she was dragging a green smudge along the banister. She trailed into the kitchen, but unsure of what she wanted to do there, flitted through to the lounge, thinking vaguely in terms of catching the last of the weekend children's programs.

Yes, that might cheer me up, she thought.

The ghost just happened to be sitting in Griswold's chair again—knitting as before. As Gemma entered, she looked up, her fingers poised in mid-stitch. Gemma's eyes widened, but the ghost's eyes bulged. They gasped in unison at the sight of each other. The ghost, having the ability, withdrew immediately, vanishing in a gentle *pop!*

Gemma stifled a scream, before running round in circles, telling herself to "Breathe! Breathe!" Used to taking orders, she obediently took two deep breaths, recovering enough to remember to contact Oswin As Soon As Possible!

Dashing through to the phone in the hall, she frantically dialled his mobile.

Chapter Six

Although Oswin answered his phone with his eyes closed, he pulled himself from his slumber instantly at the sound of Gemma's urgent voice.

"What—the ghost? Again? Where? Oh, right, I'll be there in a flash."

Of course, he literally was. He came stumbling down the stairs in his pyjamas, the ghost detector and his notebook in his grasp, the visual gadget on his head. Gemma gulped nervously at the sight of his equipment. Her green pallor got no reaction from Oswin; indeed, he was so focused on getting results from his head sensor and his handheld sensor that he barely noticed.

"Right, show me..." he said, pulling the visor down. He was plunged instantly into his private, self-created void. Seeing only shadowy darkness, he stumbled forward, stretching his arms out in an effort to detect where he was. "Oops! Ouch! Show me where the lounge is!"

Gemma took one of his hands and lead him through to the living room.

"Shall I take the hand set's readings for you?" she asked, removing the pad and hand device from him and setting to work. "This is really good. Look how high it is!"

Of course Oswin couldn't look. He stumbled around with his hands outstretched. "This way?" he asked, before swivelling round. "Or this side? I can't see!"

Absently, Gemma took him by the shoulders and turned him to face where the ghost had sat a mere minute or two ago. "Mind the chair," she said, as turned back to her recordings.

"Yes! Yes!" yelled Oswin, racing blindly towards a misty haze he glimpsed momentarily through the darkness. "Yes, I can...Oh, no I can't. I thought... Ow! No! Ow!" he groaned, tripping over the chair, and sprawling over the coffee table.

"Yes! Ha, ha! Got you!" laughed Gemma, punching the buttons of the hand detector excitedly.

Griswold arrived in the doorway just at that moment. Having been disturbed by the excitement downstairs, he had arisen from his bed, and hurried down to investigate. He froze, gaping in shock and horror at the bizarre goings on before him.

"What's all this? Gemma, what are you doing to him?"

Oswin, letting go of his shin, which he had knocked on the table in the fall, tried to get the headgear off of him. It stuck fast.

"Get it off! Oof!" Oswin groaned from beneath the helmet.

Gemma's teeth glowed hideous and bright against her green face as she grinned. Her shining eyes unnerved her father.

"What are you doing to him?" he gasped, making a grab for the hand detector. He assumed it was linked to the helmet, which was—as far as he could make out—obviously torturing Oswin. Slowly and painfully.

"You're hurting him—you're going to kill him!" cried Griswold, his voice raised to a screech. He heard Oswin's breathing behind the visor; it was laboured.

"Gemma! Please! I can't breath!" wheezed Oswin, floundering in the air with his hands as though he were drowning. Desperation tinged his voice, making it pitch to a squeal. "Gemma!"

"Huh? Oh, sorry!" said Gemma at last. "No, Dad, don't touch the buttons! Dad!" She thrust the ghost detector down the front of her dress, where Griswold's hands would never dare to go, and set to work at helping Oswin.

"What are you kids doing?" gasped Griswold, holding his head in his hands. "Can't you press one of your buttons on your remote, Gemma?" He stepped forward, making weak attempts to help with removing the helmet.

Gemma blinked and uttered an indeterminable reply as she tugged at the helmet, making Oswin squeak hoarsely. Then the helmet popped off, revealing a red-faced, panting Oswin. Griswold took a step back as he observed the blue tinge around his nephew's mouth, and the flecks of spittle on his cheeks.

Then he rounded on Gemma, his eyes bulging. "What on earth were you doing, girl?" he wheezed and pointed at the hand-held detector peeping out of her scooped neckline. "You've nearly killed him!"

Gemma frowned. "What?"

"Oh no, Uncle," Oswin explained, breathlessly at first. "That's not a remote control Gemma's holding, it's a nifty little gadget that takes readings of magnetic, static and temperature fluctuations. Part of my science practical for this term. I made it."

Griswold stared from one teenage to the other in a moment of calm confusion.

"And the helmet thingy that he was wearing is similar," Gemma joined in. "It shows the magnetic fields around objects, I think. Something like that. It's for ghost detection."

There was another pause after which Griswold whispered, "Ghost?"

Oswin swallowed. "That's right, Uncle Griswold, I'm going to prove—or disprove—the existence of ghosts. That's part of my project."

"Is it, indeed?"

"I think we may find that they really do exist," Gemma beamed supportively. "And if anyone can, our Oswin can!" She pranced about with glee, doing a neat little pirouette.

Griswold made a futile attempt at swatting her and his customary scowl deepened, darkened.

"Keep still, girl! There's no such thing as ghosts! You'll soon find out, with all your scientific gobbledygook paraphernalia that there's no such thing!"

"Then, with all due respect, sir," said Oswin quietly, "you'll let me carry on with my project without trying to stop me. I'll prove you right, if, of course, you are right!"

"There's *no such thing as ghosts!* And these gadgets look positively dangerous. This helmet especially—you nearly suffocated. No, my boy, I'm confiscating it! And this ghost-proving rubbish must stop, do you hear?" With that he snatched the helmet from Oswin and spun round to go. Oswin let him take the helmet. At least he still had...

"The remote!" spat Griswold, turning back. He stared at its hiding place, his hands clenching and unclenching but he did not lunge for the device.

"If I ever see that hand device in action again, I'm not only going to confiscate it, I'm going to smash it up!" he snarled, and turned on his heel once more.

Then he hesitated as he considered interrupting his authoritarian exit—again—to enquire why Gemma was painted green. He should have said something earlier, but it had seemed a trivial detail in the moments he thought his daughter had been torturing his nephew to death. And now, it seemed the opportunity for tackling the issue had passed. Then again, to say nothing would be to condone this strange fashion. What would be next, he wondered, Beryl in *Teletubby* yellow?

"And wash that stuff off your face, girl," he snarled at last. "You look hideous!"

"Daddy, I was hoping I could..." Gemma began timidly, her

hands fluttering like leaves blown about in a storm.

"Now, I said!" Griswold interrupted.

"Wear it to the party, as my..."

"*Now!*" he shrieked. "It's *disgusting!*"

"But Daddy, I want to wear it to Rebecca's party," Gemma pleaded.

"You're not going out of the house looking like that, my girl. And that's final!"

The look on Griswold's face was positively dangerous as he strode out with stormy determination. Then he popped his heard round the door again, and waved the helmet ominously at them.

"I'm confiscating this weird gizmo contraption, and I'm going to destroy it," he announced with a victorious sneer.

Gemma wilted, motionless in a little spotlight of misery.

"Actually," said Oswin, when Griswold's footsteps had faded upstairs, "I think it's a brilliant costume. Princess Fiona in *Shrek*, right?"

She nodded, as the first of her tears rolled down her cheek, leaving a flesh-colored path for the rest to follow on.

"See?" smiled Oswin. "I knew immediately who you were. When's the party?"

"The what?" gulped Gemma, wiping her eyes on the back of her hand.

"The fancy dress party?"

"Oh! Er...not for ages. I...er...was just trying it out, like. Er...to see if it works. I thought no one would mind if I pottered about the house like this." Gemma probably would have burst into a flood of tears, but a searing pain in her eyes took her mind off her emotional angst. She rubbed them automatically, which made the pain worse. "Look," she said, her voice strained, "the green paint is burning my eyes. I'd better wash it off. But before I go, I think the ghost saw me. She seemed astonished, frightened, almost and then she disappeared."

Oswin raised his eyebrows. "Really? Has she ever done that before?"

"I don't know. I've never waited around long enough to see. Anyway, this is really burning!" she said, pressing her hands to her bloodshot, streaming eyes as she fumbled for the door. "I'll meet you in the kitchen in a bit, yeah?"

* * * *

As soon as she had washed her face and hands to their usual pale hue, and soothed her eyes with cotton wool dipped in milk, Gemma sat with Oswin in the kitchen, discussing the morning's events over coffee and biscuits.

"Well, even if the head gear is a big flop, the hand device measures the fields very well," remarked Oswin. "The readings are almost down to normal, now."

"I think you're brilliant to have it work so well on the first prototype." Gemma beamed, removing the cotton wool pads from her eyes. They were still a bit red, but they'd stopped watering.

Oswin blushed and coughed. "Pity we can't say the same about the head gear."

"Don't be so negative! If you keep on working at it, you'll iron out all the..."

Gemma stopped and blinked and stared at the washing machine. The back of her neck prickled. The machine had been puttering along nicely through a delicate cycle. As it began to spin suddenly at its full 12 000 revolutions, a shadow bounded from its vicinity and streaked over their heads to vanish somewhere by the wall clock.

Gemma and Oswin ducked instinctively as though a wasp had dived at them from nowhere. The ghost detector set off in a volley of pips and static squeals. Oswin later swore he saw a second shadow closely following the first.

"Did you see that?" he breathed as they stared at each other, both pale and shaking. Gemma let out a sob, her hands darted between her mouth and her chest. But in a moment she collected herself enough to remember they were supposed to be recording this sort of thing. She grappled with pen and pages as Oswin, picking up her cue, shakily read out the reading.

"It hates us, I can feel it," Gemma whispered. "The housewife ghost is...just there, in comparison. But this, whatever it is, *loathes* us."

Oswin stared at the meter. He ran his fingers through his hair and sighed, "I dunno, this seems wrong. The readings are dropping much quicker than before."

"Is it...is it malfunctioning?"

There was a long silence. Gemma played with the cotton wool pads, squeezing drops of milk out on the table, while Oswin fiddled with the detector. At last he said, "Well, I'll run some tests, then probably rebuild it, anyway. Like you said, it's only the prototype, after all. I think I'd better disguise it as a toy of some sort.

That ought to fool Griswold and Beryl. It shouldn't take long; it took just a couple of days to build this one. And the helmet—well that needed to be rebuilt anyway."

There was another pause as Oswin studied the gadget again, pressing buttons here and there.

"Oh, well," he said at last, "it's probably malfunctioning. The readings are already back to normal. Far too early according to the earlier incidents!"

"But Oswin," Gemma replied in a hushed voice, "that wasn't the ghost I usually see. Not at all."

"Are you sure?"

Gemma nodded. "I told you. This wasn't the housewife. I've seen her before often enough. She's got a totally different...*feel* about her. This was something different...a shadowy thing. I felt it more than saw it. Don't you sometimes wake up in the night and feel it lurking about upstairs? I always assumed it was the same ghost, but maybe..." her voice trailed to a whisper. "Maybe there's more than one ghost."

Oswin folded his arms, then pushed his glasses higher along the bridge of his nose and nodded. "Hmm...It's either the same ghost in different moods, or two separate entities," he said at last. "And one's a lot nastier than the other."

Chapter Seven

A lull in any sightings over the next few days allowed Gemma to relax once again and Oswin used the time to get on with his next prototype. Gemma kept forgetting this was a school project and, feeling guilty at all the work her cousin was going through on her behalf, she did what she could to help. She named the handheld ghost detector the 'Ghost-O-Meter', covered the diary in wrapping paper and wrote in it every day, even if it was just to say "nothing strange today." She brought him up mugs of coffee, stopping sometimes to chat a while too.

"It's nice to have someone agree with me that this house always has funny things happening in it," she remarked as she lay on Oswin's bed, tracing dance steps on the wall with her sock-clad feet. He was putting the finishing touches to his next 'Ghost-O-Meter.'

"You mean, 'unexplained'?" he corrected, without pausing in his work.

"Exactly! Like when the fridge defrosted on its own."

"Your dad said one of us must have accidentally flicked the switch off and we thought it was him."

"But we know it wasn't any of us and who's to say *he* really did it, like we thought?" said Gemma. "Plus when you add up all the times the geyser's been mysteriously turned up—and down! And the times the tap in the bathroom just starts dripping, as though someone turned it on..."

"Or didn't turn it off properly..." muttered Oswin, as he dropped a silvery liquid ball onto a chip board.

"Aw, come on! We all turn it off properly. Things just go missing in this house then turn up weeks later in odd places."

"Yeah," Oswin agreed sceptically. "But it could just be that we're a careless bunch. Which reminds me, Beryl was going on about a Coast sweater she's lost. She wanted to go through my cupboards..."

"Remember that time you thought we had burglars because the toilet had just flushed as you came home—and the house was empty?"

Oswin stopped his work, soldering iron in his hand. Only

Gemma had believed his account of the flushing loo.

"Yeah, right," he said. "Spooky, that was." Frowning, he bent over the chipboard again. "Perhaps we should take a reading whenever that sort of thing happens."

"It may either prove or disprove that poltergeist theory."

"Although, ghosts of the spectral sort—I can swallow that, but a poltergeist...mm...I dunno, so much."

Oswin consulted some notes then worked in silence for a while, as they both mused over the possibilities, then he said, "Of course, it *is* consistent with the ley line theory: the idea that different types supernatural anomalies are...er...*attracted* to this place."

Gemma arched her eyebrows. "Like I said the other day—more than one type of ghost?"

"That's right, there may be more than we've bargained for." Oswin's eyes brightened with a new idea. "They may come and go, for all we know. Fascinating!"

"Okay...I could add another column in the ghost diary, for when strange things happen. What shall I call it? Poltergeist? Gremlins...?" She sat up cross-legged on the bed and reached for the ghost diary and a pen.

"Mm, good idea. But I think something more scientific would look better on my project."

They debated the issue for a while and eventually settled for Unexplained Influential Phenomena or U.I.P. although Gemma thought that Poltergeist would have sounded nicer. She sucked her pen absently as she recalled many odd happenings that she had shrugged off as her imagination, one after the other. Perhaps it was her frame of mind at that moment, but she thought she could hear movement—some activity—downstairs.

Looking at Oswin, she whispered, "Did you hear that?"

"Mmm?" he answered absently, busy aiming melting drops of wire on the board.

Gemma paused, wondering whether or not to tell him to stop and listen to the movements downstairs. Considering their immediate discussion, she knew he would assume she was over reacting. He would say so, insist that they check and then, on finding none of his *'paranormal activity,'* he would have her note it down in the records book as a false alarm. Due to her being unnerved.

So she changed her tune somewhat. "Coffee?" she offered.

"Mm...Ta!"

Gemma jumped up and, surreptitiously keeping the records book with her, tiptoed down to the kitchen. Oh, yes, from now on she was going to investigate every one of her suspicions, take them seriously and not assume that it was all down to her imagination. Every creaking noise in the old house, every shadow that flittered, was going to be explained or marked down as officially unexplained.

As Gemma neared the bottom of the stairs, her heart leaped into her throat and clung there, thudding wildly. There was definitely movement in the kitchen. Edging nearer, she recognized the sound of the kettle being filled. Numbness began to crawl over her as images of what spectre might be lurking with the kettle in its hand flickered through her mind, but with her first glance at the source of the noise, Gemma's heart slid down to its proper position with a plop. She felt a fool, for having not realized that the noises were the clumsy movements of Beryl.

"Oh," she said. "I see...er..."

"I can't help you with anything now," warned Beryl flatly. "I'm in the middle of studying. With Ronnie!"

From Beryl's flushing cheeks, the coy toss of her head, Gemma surmised that Ronnie was a bloke.

"I was just coming to make some coffee," she said lamely, hanging back in the doorway.

"Well, you'll have to wait. I'm busy here!" Beryl hardly looked at Gemma as she spoke, and bustled about with a sense of urgency, flinging cupboard doors open and slamming them shut again. "Where's the cream? Don't we have some coffee cream?"

"In the fridge," Gemma said.

"In those little individual pots, like in the restaurant?"

"In the fridge, I said."

Beryl finally accepted this, and rushed to the fridge, bustling Gemma aside. "Mind out the way!"

She hung onto the fridge door, peering inside, and muttering, "Hmm...what's this...It should have been chucked out ages ago...Ah—here it is...wait a minute!" Beryl reached in behind the mayonnaise and pulled out half of a six pack of cider. She grinned wickedly as she held it aloft. "Aha! This is way better than coffee."

"Not for studying it isn't," said Gemma quietly.

Beryl's selective hearing clicked into action and, humming to herself, she fetched two glasses and re-applied her lip-gloss.

"Perhaps cans will be better, more spontaneous," she said, pausing in the doorway. "Glasses may be too posh. You know, we *are* students after all. What do you think?"

"Coffee! Really, I think coffee is best."

Beryl seemed to consider this for a moment.

"Um...Yeah, right...impromptu. Yes!" She put the glasses down and called to Ronnie as she went upstairs, "Sorry Ronnie, we're out of cream...and coffee. But I've found a nice alternative!"

"Okay," said Gemma to the doorway, as the kettle began to whistle. "So, can I use the water?"

Beryl did not hear Gemma's plaintive calls; she was too busy checking her reflection in the bathroom mirror before entering her boudoir. Chuckling to herself, she picked her way over books and papers and wedged herself close beside a dark haired boy of seventeen. He wore glasses, but had a square jaw and a sensuous mouth—fit for any hero—and although he seemed gangly, beneath his loose shirt gym grown muscles were rippling.

"Ah, sweet!" he said, looking up at her. His eyes were an unusual shade of hazel, almost yellow. They looked like the eyes of a tiger.

Beryl opened the first can with a crack and a fizz. "Now," she said huskily, "run that theory by me again."

Ronnie shifted uncomfortably and began...

Chapter Eight

Gemma looked nervously at Beryl's closed door as she carried two mugs of coffee with cream upstairs.

"Beryl's drinking," she told Oswin as she set coffee down. "And I mean, proper drink. Cider."

"Well, she is eighteen, Gem," he pointed out, cricking his back with a deft movement of his shoulders, then taking up his mug. "Thanks! It's allowed, isn't it?"

"Not by Dad, it isn't."

"She'll never allow herself to be caught out!"

Gemma leaned in, deep concern furrowing her brows. "But there's a boy from her college. She's got him in there and the door's shut. And they're drinking."

Oswin considered this for a moment. "I thought they were supposed to be studying."

"Exactly! And so does he, I think. But now she's trying to seduce him with drink. What if she gets her way?"

"Ugh!" Oswin shuddered. "Don't speak such hideous thoughts out loud. Not when I'm trying to drink my coffee." Why did girls always have to bring sex into everything, he wondered?

"Yeah, but what if she succeeds?"

"She won't."

"And Dad catches them…"

"Stop it!" Oswin set his mug down and rounded sternly on Gemma. "She won't! He won't! Beryl would never let herself get caught at anything. She is very scheming, you know. Always in control. Plus she won't be thinking of—ugh!—*that* now. She's frantic about the mock exams."

Gemma shook her head, "You didn't see her in the kitchen! But I did and I know what she's planning."

Oswin sighed and stared at his cousin. "Fine!" he said at last. "Beryl's in her room and she's drinking and snogging some poor, unsuspecting bloke. But, you know what? It's not my concern. I'm busy working on my term project. And I suggest you find something to keep your mind off what your sister is up to in the privacy of her own room."

He gave her a stern look and turned back to his work. Gemma

sat and stared ahead at nothing. After a pause Oswin said, without looking up, "By the way, thanks for the coffee. It's nice."

"I'd better get on with my homework," Gemma sighed, getting up. She left his room slowly, with a couple of backward glances but he was too busy looking from sheets of diagrams to his construction to notice her. She sighed again and walked out in a slow ballet march. On the landing, she heard a muffled cry coming from Beryl's room. She hovered by the door, unable to bring herself to move on, listening...

* * * *

"Give it back!" commanded Beryl in her room, her eyes glowing.

"I told you! I ain't got it!" cried Ronnie, squirming, as she tried to frisk him. Her fingers dug in everywhere, like a series of ramrods poking at his ribs.

"Aaah! No! I'm ticklish!" he shrieked, trying to ward her off with flailing arms, but she lunged with more determination, knocking him down and kneeling on top of him.

"Cut it out!" he shrieked, squirming and trying to un-trap his left arm. "Aaah! No, Beryl! You're freaking me out!"

* * * *

Outside the room, Gemma leaned closer to the door to hear better...

* * * *

Ronnie struggled free, threw himself at the door—making poor Gemma jump back in fright—and grabbing at the handle, but the door wouldn't open.

"What the? You...you've locked the door!" he cried, whipping round to face his assailant. With his back against the door, he stared at Beryl in disbelief. She took advantage of his moment of disarmed surprise and lunged at him again.

"Come 'ere you!"

Panic stricken, he shoved her roughly away and, running over her bed, reached the window—safety—before she could pick herself up. He jumped out.

"*Aaaah!*" Ronnie's screams rebounded down the street as he hurtled from the second story window down into a flower bed full of shrubs and rose bushes. For a moment he lay in frightening stillness. The world paused in freeze-frame, waiting, then he twitched.

"Aaah! Jeez!" he wheezed as he picked himself up and scrambled out. Something rigid thudded onto him, grasping him by the upper arm, squeezing painfully at his knotted muscles with a deep, menacing snarl.

"What's this?"

Griswold's hands closed in even tighter on Ronnie, making him twist and shriek as he yanked the lad out of the bushes with an alarmingly powerful tug, as though pulling weeds.

He put his face close to Ronnie's who quivered, pale and bleeding, like a vole in the jaws of cat.

"What were you doing to my daughter?"

"Sir...Please, man!" Ronnie's head flopped about limply as Griswold's shook him roughly, fireworks of pain cart-wheeling around his various scratches and bruises. A cold sweat of pinpricks scurried over his flesh as nausea swelled up inside him like a flood behind a damn wall. And it broke.

"What the..." Griswold gasped and fell into a fuchsia bush in the attempt to get his feet out of the way, as Ronnie bent over double, his body racked in spasms.

Griswold watched Ronnie heave and heave again.

"You're drunk, lad!" he snarled scornfully.

"*Father, no!* Ronnieeee!"

Beryl's cries came from her window. "Father! *You beast!* What have you done to him? Hold on, Ronnie, I'm coming!"

Griswold blinked, glanced around then, staring upwards, declared, "I never touched him!" But Beryl's face had gone from the window. She was thundering down the stairs.

Ronnie, sensing his attacker's distraction, gathered what strength he could muster and zigzagged out of the front garden, down the street to the bus stop, praying every stumbling step of the way that a bus would be there.

Griswold let him go and rounded on his eldest daughter as she charged out of the front door, one arm outstretched and the other clutched at her breast. She would have followed Ronnie, but Griswold jumped in front of her, barring her way.

"I want to know what's been going on here!" he snarled. "I come home a little early and I find everyone drunk as lords and some Casanova leaping from the windows. It's a wonder you've all got your clothes on!"

"*Father!*"

Griswold looked about. Net curtains were twitching all down the street. "Get into the house!"

"No!" roared Beryl with melodramatic gusto. "I want the world to know, it's not true..."

Griswold bundled her clumsily through the door. It was a difficult task, and took a good few moments of embarrassing struggle, because apart from Beryl's large size, she kept trying to wedge her arms and legs in the doorway to prevent him from pushing her through. Oswin was called down to help pry her limbs off the door frame, one at a time, and shove them to her side. It was a bit like trying to pin down a flailing octopus. Eventually, she succumbed, and popped through the doorway like a fleshy cork, with Griswold falling indoors after her.

He slammed the door shut and leaned on it, panting, unaware that Oswin was tapping timidly from outside, asking to be let in. Beryl collapsed on her hands and knees, wailing and shaking her head despairingly.

Griswold goggled at her. "What has gotten into you?"

"I...I...love him!" Sobbing miserably, she sat up on her haunches. "But he doesn't know. He only came here to help me study. Then he suddenly wanted to go..." She paused to wail pitifully for a moment. "But the door wouldn't open. He thought it was locked and...he thought I had locked him in. But I didn't, Father, I didn't!"

"You lured a man into your room under false pretences of studying so that you could lock him in and have your way with him?" Griswold spluttered.

"No! Father, how *could* you? Look at me!" She did look a sight, with red eyes, smudged mascara and dishevelled hair. "Look at me! Would I ever do such a terrible thing?"

Now that the question was put to him, Griswold had to admit. No. That was too farfetched to be true.

"I think he'd been drinking before he arrived," covered Beryl, quickly regaining some of her posture and even finding the strength to stand up—unsteadily of course. "Yes, that's it! I think he'd had a few, which is shocking really when he's been invited to a study session, to have been consuming alcohol. But nevertheless, he *had* been drinking, which is why he overreacted when the door wouldn't open. Yes, that's it! He thought he was locked in and panicked. Oh, and he broke the curtain rail jumping out."

"Why didn't you study in the dining room?" asked Griswold, after a moment's digestion.

"I...er...It's a bit cold in that room, actually. Besides, I'm so used to studying in my room..."

"Well, next time, hold your study parties in the dining room!"

Having found a point where he could draw the matter to an official close and recuperate in peace, Griswold started forward to go to the front room and pour himself a large whisky.

Beryl pushed passed Gemma, who was sitting on the bottom of the stairs, and ran up to her room. Like Oswin, Gemma had gone unnoticed throughout this interview. She was scribbling something in her ghost diary.

"Time: 5:03 p.m. Date: 10th October. Incident: Beryl's bedroom door locked/jammed. She did not lock it. I was not leaning on it. The door mysteriously unlocked/jammed moments later, when she opened it. She did not pause to unlock it and had no trouble in opening it.

Explanation: It may have been jammed but there has never been trouble like that with her door before. She would have made a fuss if she had a sticky door."

Having finished her logging, Gemma got up and opened the front door to let in Oswin—who had given up knocking and was standing patiently on the doorstep with his arms folded.

"What a bleeding pantomime!" he growled and stomped past her up to his room.

Gemma hovered at the bottom of the stairs. The fancy dress party was only four weeks away and she still hadn't had an official yes from Griswold. She had been planning to ask him afresh if she could go. This was not a good time but her impatience kept her in the hall. She found herself practising her latest dance routine, in little understated steps, counting with her breathing. "One...two... three...four....up...two...over...d-r-a-g...two..."

Someone brushed passed her. Absorbed in her routine, she glanced over her shoulder as she continued. Nothing. A rush of gooseflesh sent her skin crawling, as she knew instantly, *certainly*, that the ghost had rushed passed her. The contact, the rustle had been real. She knew, by the direction of the movement, the culprit had gone to the front room. As she looked up she should have seen whoever it was turning into the front room. But there was no one. Nothing. Just cold, icy stillness.

With a stifled cry, Gemma bounded up the stairs. Oswin was putting the final touches to the Ghost-O-Meter when she plunged into his room, her heart still thudding wildly.

"Oswin, I've just felt it. The ghost. On the stairs!"

He looked up from his work, screwdriver in hand, "Darn!" he breathed. He looked at the Ghost-O-Meter and back at her, shrugged apologetically, "Sorry Gem! It's not screwed together yet. Record the sighting in the book and mark it as unread," he said, driving little screws into their holes. "I'll measure the area as soon as I get this done. Shouldn't lose too much time. Was it the housewife as usual?"

"I don't know. I felt it go passed but didn't see anything," said Gemma,

"Ah!" Oswin paused to look up again. "A kinesthetic encounter."

"I know what I felt. I'd just had Beryl and then you brush past me, and then this third...I was even thinking, funny how things happen in threes, and I looked up to see who it was. But there was no one."

"I believe you," said Oswin enthusiastically. "It even makes the haunting idea more plausible. The sort of encounter you've just experienced is the more common sort. Most people feel and hear things, rather than see them."

Gemma blinked. "Oh, right," she mumbled and opened her ghost diary.

Chapter Nine

Beryl went into a deep and official fit of depression over Ronnie. She stayed shut up in her room, which was the nice part of her mourning. Then, after three days, when no one but Gemma came in—and that was only to give her meals on a tray—she ventured out. She sniffed and wiped her eyes in front of everyone. Griswold had prepared a shabby lunch for the family and they picked at it in silence. Silence apart, that is, from Beryl's occasional sniff followed by watery sighs.

At last Griswold groaned and rolled his eyes. "Aw, you're not still crying over that boy, are you?"

"Yes I am, not that you care!" Beryl said, welling up again. She dropped her fork with a clatter and pushed a paper napkin to her face.

"You'll get over him in time. It's no use chasing a bloke down, Beryl," advised Griswold, patting her uncomfortably on her shoulder. "They don't like it. It scares them half to death. You set your heart on someone who likes you, pet, and you'll get a better response."

Beryl gave an indignant chirp and glared at him over the serviette. "Ha! I did *not* chase him down. Never!" She sobbed enthusiastically, drenching the napkin. "Don't you understand? I've given my heart to him. That's it! There's never going to be another man in my life..."

Oswin and Gemma caught each other's eye. That was a mistake. Trying to quell their laughter they grinned, red faced, into their plates. One or two snorts erupted into the tense atmosphere and, luckily, went unchallenged.

"It's only been a couple of days," said Griswold.

"It's been three days, and two hours and six minutes," wailed Beryl. "You wouldn't notice if I'd died!"

"Now don't talk like that, Beryl, not in front of the little ones! Besides, of course I'd notice. I need you back to your old self. No one can cook as well as you. The dinners have been dismal since you..."

"You *need* me but you don't *care!*" said Beryl, her eyes blazing, "or you wouldn't have sent him away."

Griswold abandoned his meal, throwing his knife and fork down. "I didn't send him away! He ran away. From *you*, no doubt."

Beryl gave a short cry of horror and clutched at her bosom, glaring at Griswold, her jaw dropped open in a gesture of shock.

"Why else did he jump out of the window?" he said.

"And you still haven't been up to my room to fix my curtain rail!" Beryl said, deftly shifting the focus of their argument. "What kind of a father would let her daughter get dressed with the whole street able to watch?" She nodded, with arched brows at Gemma and Oswin, trying to evoke their support.

Griswold put his head in his hands, "Alright, alright!"

"I'm not cooking another meal for you, until you've mended my curtain rail!" Beryl said.

She threw her fork down and stomped up the stairs, banging her bedroom door and leaving the rest of the family sitting around the table in a silent, tense trio.

Within minutes, Griswold scraped his chair back and trudged up the stairs to examine the broken rail. Beryl languished on her bed, watching him from beneath her puffy, half-mast eyes.

"And while you're at it," she said, "the toilet's blocked or something."

"Hmm...?" he replied absently, with his hands on his hips, staring at the fittings. "I'm going to have to go to Wicks to get a part."

"Can't I have a whole new rail? That one makes me think of *him* every time I look at it. Oh! And it hurts so much, Father!" Beryl broke into fresh weeping.

"Mm..." Griswold's focus remained on the rail, until at last he managed to tear himself from the task at hand. "There, there, pet, don't cry!" He came over and patted her shoulder. "I'll have to get a whole new rail, I think."

With a tap on the door, Gemma popped her head into the room. "Ah, Dad, while you've got your tool box out, the toilet isn't flushing properly—could you have a look at it?"

"Alright, alright! Cor Blimey! You kids treat me like I'm a landlord the minute I have my tools out." Griswold grumbled, crossing the landing to look at the toilet.

"Oh, and Beryl," Gemma said, "there's a man on the phone for you. He says he's..."

Beryl sprang from the bed and pushing Gemma out of the way, sprinted onto the landing in a single motion, bounding down the stairs to the hall.

"What the hell have you kids been up to!" barked Griswold,

from the W.C. "Beryl, Gemma, Oswin, come here *now!*"

"Who's done this?" he demanded, as Gemma and Oswin stepped into view. He reached into the cistern and pulled out a pink, sodden mass.

Gemma gasped. "That's Beryl's sweater! Her Coast sweater. She's been looking for it for ages!"

"Well, who the blazers put it here?"

Gemma and Oswin shrugged blankly. They looked at each other in bemusement then back at Griswold, holding the pink, dribbling bundle.

"Come on, who's the prankster?" he asked again, focusing on Oswin.

"It wasn't us!"

"Well, it didn't crawl in here by itself."

"It was *not us!*" Oswin repeated, his steel eyes glinting behind his spectacles. Griswold surveyed him narrowly. Oswin held his ground.

"Daddy, this is insane," said Gemma. "None of us would do such a crazy thing." Then her eyes lit up, "Ah! I know! Daddy, don't you see? This is ghostly activity..."

"Don't be daft!" Griswold cut her off. "You'd better see to this!" He plonked the dripping sweater into her arms with a squelch, "Beryl's going to be..."

"Be what?" asked Beryl, having appeared on the landing. Then she gasped—long and loud and very meaningful. Like the hiss of an emptying balloon. Gemma cringed in the following lull.

"My Coast sweater! Who's done this? Who's put my sweater down the loo? It's cashmere!" Beryl shrieked. She boxed Oswin's ears and caught Gemma a blow over her head too. "Which one of you imps have...."

"Beryl no!" yelled Griswold. "You are not to hit kids nowadays! You're not to touch them. It's all reasoning and punishment, remember? Rewards and consequences! Spite is your only weapon!"

Beryl took a deep, noisy, breath. "Right!" she snapped. "This is the work of one of you two."

"Actually, I think we have a polter..." began Oswin.

"And you two can restore it to its former glory, or buy me another one! It cost me over fifty quid." Beryl turned to Griswold. "Fair enough?"

He nodded.

"It wasn't us!" Gemma protested, bobbing nervously.

"I," Beryl continued haughtily, "am going out. I am meeting

Ronnie's mate. We're going to chat about the other day. I am going to clear my name. And perhaps find some comfort at last into the bargain. I insisted we meet in a public place for various reasons, safety being one of them, so don't try to stop me! I can look after myself, thank you, Father. Get out of my way, you two, I've got to wash my hair before I go out."

Beryl shoved Gemma and Oswin aside so hard they bumped their heads on the wall, as she stalked into the bathroom, slamming the door with a furious bang!

"You heard her," said Griswold after a pause. "Get that sweater sorted. I'm going to Wicks."

"But it wasn't us," Gemma said, as Griswold hurried down the stairs.

"Come on Gem," Oswin said. "No one's listening. And this is definitely one you can put in your ghost diary!"

Chapter Ten

Oswin and Gemma carried the sweater downstairs, squeezed it out and washed it with a detergent for delicates. Gemma felt compelled to look over her shoulder a couple of times, but apart from the feeling of being watched, she had to admit there was no ghostly interference.

To dry the sweater after its ordeal they wrapped it in an old towel and trod on it. They took turns at this and had a little fun with it, jumping and pretending to do a Russian dance.

Then Gemma got the softest hairbrush she could find and brushed the sweater gently until it had a fine hairy sheen all around it.

"I'll just run the new Ghost Meter over that sweater before you put it in the airing cupboard," Oswin said. "You never know. By the way, there must be some other ghost. That old housewife you describe doesn't seem the sort to throw delicates in the toilet cistern."

"No, she doesn't," Gemma smiled, enjoying brushing the sweater. It was like having a pet. "Do you think it's a poltergeist? They move stuff around, don't they?"

Oswin ran his fingers through his hair. "Dunno," he replied and left to fetch the Ghost-O-Meter. He hoped not, actually. From what he'd read, many cases of poltergeist activity involved a young girl in the throws of puberty. The suppressed sort, quiet and obedient on the outside, burning with rage on the inside. From what he'd read, these girls seemed to be linked with the eerie activity. They were often seen as targets of the ghost then later, as such cases unfolded, they were accused of instigating all the thumps and bumps and flying articles. Could this be a similar case? Could Gemma really turn out to be a fraud? Oswin hated the thought.

"I think the old housewife spook would be well pleased with my efforts," Gemma said proudly when he returned with the ghost-o-meter. She was laying the sweater flat in the airing cupboard.

"Hey, I wonder if Beryl didn't chuck her sweater in the cistern as a way of getting you to wash it for her."

Gemma laughed. "Don't be daft! This sweater is precious to her. She always has it dry-cleaned."

"Yeah, I suppose you're right," Oswin sighed. "I guess I was just grasping at straws."

"I wonder where she is, though. She's taking ages to 'clear her name' with what's-his-name."

"That's our Beryl," Oswin said dryly. He ran the Ghost-O-Meter over the pink, fluffy mass. "Nope, the sweater's clear. But it's soaked in cold water for Heaven knows how long and then been washed." He turned the meter over in his hand, fiddling with a couple of dials. It was a bigger, smarter version than the last.

"It looks just like a gun," remarked Gemma. "Like a toy space gun."

Oswin grinned. "Exactly! That's what I used as a basic frame. Griswold and Beryl will never guess—they'll think I'm playing when, in fact, I'm taking readings." He stroked the Ghost-O-Meter's long barrel. It had LEDs running along the side.

"It's very professional," Gemma said, pirouetting neatly to punctuate the compliment. "It looks like a good quality toy."

Oswin smiled proudly. It was well worth the great chunk he had spent out of his money to buy the parts.

"When it detects something, these will light up."

The phone rang, loud and shrill, cutting through their conversation. Gemma ran to pick it up. It was Griswold on the other end of the line, and he told her that he'd bumped into another of their cousins—a grown up, recently married nephew who's company he rather enjoyed.

"I'm a bit delayed," he told Gemma. "I've met our Bruce down at Wicks, believe it or not, and I've gone back to their house to help with mending their bathroom taps. It seems Sally got her big toe caught in the cold tap, and they had to break it in order to free her," he chuckled. "So, I don't know when I'll be back. Put Beryl on, I want to tell her Bruce invited us round for Sunday lunch."

Griswold seemed so happy and relaxed that Gemma deduced he'd had a couple of Guinness' with Bruce.

"Beryl's not back yet," she replied.

"Not?"

"No. I suppose she'll be back any minute. I'll pass your message on to her."

Gemma relayed the conversation to Oswin in his room as he jotted concluding notes on his handheld gadget down. She did a double pirouette when, glancing over his shoulder, she saw that he referred to the gizmo officially as a Ghost-O-Meter. As she was following her victory gesture through with a series of hand movements, she heard something on the landing—floor boards creaking.

"Ah! That must be Beryl now," she said and went to give her Griswold's message.

Oswin followed her out, running downstairs to take a general, neutral reading of the house with his new Ghost-O-Meter. He started in the front room and worked his way efficiently through to the back and the landing.

Gemma met him at the bottom of the stairs. "Beryl isn't in her room after all, nor in the bathroom or the loo. Is she down here?"

Oswin shook his head.

"I must have imagined hearing her."

"Or it was the pipes, or something," Oswin said absently, his eyes on the meter readings. "Yeah, get the book and enter that all readings were normal at this time. We'll begin our watch again," he continued as they started up the stairs. "The meter's working fine."

He pointed the Ghost-O-Meter at the landing, as though shooting aimlessly. The sound display, adapted from the original toy gun's effects, puttered weakly and the lights along the side flashed briefly. There was a slight pause.

"Hang on, what's this?" he breathed. "The readings are higher here."

Chapter Eleven

Oswin immediately took the Ghost-O-Meter up to his room and examined it carefully. He sighed and ran his fingers through his hair. "I don't know. I suppose, before giving this new Ghost-O-Meter up as a flop, we should take readings on the landing at ten-minute intervals for an hour or so. That'll show if it's working or not."

And six readings later, when Gemma showed him the recordings, their efforts were rewarded.

"They're coming down steadily," said Oswin, looking in the ghost diary. "But we've got no sighting to go with it."

"Unless you count my hearing someone on the landing," Gemma said, chewing the top of her pencil.

"Yes, of course! We thought that was Beryl coming in. Most ghostly activities are unexplained noises. People just write them off as imagined, or the creaking of an old building, or..."

"Or the pipes?"

"Exactly!"

Just then the phone rang again and Gemma scrambled to answer it. This time it was Beryl.

"Gemma, thank Gawd!" gushed Beryl. Her voice was thicker, slower than usual. It unnerved Gemma. "I'm in a terrible scrape! I need you to come and get me." She spluttered or coughed, as though fighting back tears.

"Where are you? What is it?" Gemma asked frantically. She'd never heard her sound quite like this before.

"I was tricked! I'm down at the Green Barrow." Beryl's reply was followed quickly by another spluttering sound.

"Down at the pub!" Gemma gasped, "Whatever are you doing there?"

"I told you, I was tricked."

Gemma could hear someone talking in the background; it sounded like a man's voice.

Beryl continued, "So, it's like, my legs won't move—from whatever. I can't walk. I'm paralysed..." Another splutter "...I think I've been spiked—poisoned....Think I've been set up...Meeting him...Nnnngh! My face is going numb!" More mutterings in the background. Gemma fancied they sounded aggressive. "...Quickly—get Father to fetch me!"

"Right," Gemma said, her heart pounding. "Dad's not here..." She was going to suggest ringing the police but Beryl gave another strange spluttering noise and the phone went dead.

Gemma stared around wildly for a moment then she hurried into Oswin's room, her feet tapping, hands fluttering as she relayed the conversation to him.

"The Green Barrow?" he said. That was the local pub. "Are you sure she's not drunk?"

"I...dunno," Gemma faulted and twirled a strand of her hair. She was sure that Beryl had been kidnapped. "I just got the impression that Beryl was in some sort of trouble..."

"She will be if your father finds out," Oswin quipped. "Come on, we'd better get her home before he gets back, or there'll be hell to pay and you'll both be grounded forever."

Gemma's eyes widened, "I hope not! The party—the fancy dress party!"

The Green Barrow was easy walking distance from the house and, hurrying along, they were there within ten minutes. Gemma rushed in, then hung back in the doorway, looking in at the unfamiliar room. It was dark, full of alcoves and corners, and furnished with wooden tables and chairs and a few claret upholstered armchairs. Little groups sat hunched over their beer glasses or leaned, propping up the high bar. Behind an arched division was a snooker table with a huddle of men glaring her way and menacingly rubbing their cue sticks as though sharpening them for a skirmish. A figure near the pool table, apparently asleep, draped itself like a dirty pile of laundry over a grubby armchair and across a little round table. The low ceiling with all its old-fashioned knick-knacks hanging on the wall made the scene seem dingier than ever. The air was rank with stale spills of beer and wine. There were the sounds of coughs and wheezes and the rumble of men's conversation. Gemma felt distinctly unwelcome. It seemed the deep hum of conversation paused while everyone and everything in the pub eyed the children out with suspicion.

"We...er...um..." Gemma spluttered, fidgeting—her feet tracing out quick little ballet steps.

"We've come to fetch her. Beryl MacPherson," Oswin said loudly. But his voice was thinner than usual.

"Oh, her," growled a voice. The children gradually made out the figure of a balding man behind the counter. "I've been trying to get her out for the last hour or so. Won't budge. Says she's paralysed. She's drunk, of course. Ran up quite a tab. Luckily I know her father. I hope he sent you with the money for it?"

"We haven't any money!" Gemma said. "Dad's not home."

"No, that's right, we don't have any money," Oswin said.

"What?" demanded the barman, towering behind the bar.

Oswin swallowed hard before adding, "And I don't know if you're legally permitted to sell her alcohol. She's not quite eighteen."

"What?" roared the barman, his eyes beginning to bulge. "She said she was almost thirty!" The pub fell silent.

The laundry heap at the little round table stirred and raised its head. "Aah ham seventeen going hon thirty!" it slurred.

Gemma and Oswin exchanged glances. It *was* Beryl.

"You bloody kids and your fake I.D.'s ! I'll have..."

Beryl talked over the barman loudly, gesturing widely with a drink in her hand, its contents sloshing out as she did so. Her booming voice cut through the pub, making the regulars hunch over their glasses, irritated scowls on their faces.

"This is mah baby sister ah was telling you about. Isn't she—*hic*—sweet? But she's the reason ah'm so awful with those man and woman games. Don't understand them see? 'Cos when—*hic*—other kids were honing their social skills ah was excluded from all that. Had to bring her up, see? Ah had no choice. Mother-God-rest-her-soul died of cancer of the lymph glands and Father-poor-soul is totally absent. He works all the time to avoid the sadness of having—*hic*—lost Mother, may-she-rest-in-eternal..."

"Beryl!" Gemma squeaked. "Beryl, stop it! How *could* you? Oh, Oswin help!"

Gemma cursed her own stupidity: All that thick-voiced slurring on the phone—how could she not have realized that Beryl was drunk? And those little spluttery gasps Beryl had made were just drunken hiccups, not sobs! What a fool she was—why hadn't she caught on straight away?

Beryl, meanwhile, stared blearily at her and blinked with an expression of innocent defensiveness. "What? Ah'm only telling the truth. You know me—tell it like it is Beryl ..."

"Yeah, in the loudest, longest possible way," Oswin mumbled. He strode over to her side. "Come on, Coz, we're taking you home." He took hold of one limp arm. "Here Gem, take the other arm."

Gemma scurried round with small agitated steps, to grasp Beryl's free arm. But she swiped at Oswin.

"As for him—the great genius won—*hic*—der boy..."

"Beryl, please!" Gemma cried, her cheeks flushing.

"Ow ma ears. Don't scream in ma ears! You hurt ma ears," Beryl slurred then sank into drunken oblivion.

The other pub guests gave a cheer,

"You kids shouldn't be in here," the barman said, advancing on them.

"And neither should she," Gemma snapped. "She's only seventeen, that's too young, isn't it?"

The barman stopped in his stride and scowled. "Not according to her I.D."

"She told me her drink was spiked," Gemma said tearfully.

"Which one?" he scoffed. "She's had at least seven. That bloke she was with bought the first two. Then he got sick of her prattling on about all her woes and wondered off. No one spiked her drinks. She's just gotten herself blind drunk in next to no time."

"Quick, get her out," his wife added, coming in from the kitchen. She was a tall, thin woman, with hair piled in a great heap on top of her head.

"Yeah," chipped in a regular. "Quick before she wakes up!"

It was obvious that Beryl was far too heavy and awkward a shape for the two kids to lug all the way home. And none of the adults really wanted to get that involved.

"Put her in the wheelbarrow," someone suggested. There was a huge green, wooden wheelbarrow, filled with potted flowers, in the front courtyard.

"Quick before she wakes up!" repeated one of the snooker players, dropping his cue and hoisting Beryl over his shoulders.

"Don't be daft!" the publican said. "That's for ornamental purposes, I doubt its wheel even turns."

The snooker player grunted breathlessly, weaving under Beryl's weight as he made unsteadily for the front door.

"Wait!" the publican's wife cried. "There's a real barrow out back!"

Beryl was in that barrow with Gemma and Oswin pushing her down the street in less time than it takes a Guinness to settle. Her legs and one arm were draped over the sides and her head bobbled about with the gentle motion of her transportation. One of the regulars had thoughtfully put a long stemmed rose between her teeth.

The journey went well and when Beryl woke, three quarters of the way home, she plucked the rose from her teeth, looked at it lovingly and began to sing a power ballad in a warbling voice, slightly off-key. She was noisy, but at least she didn't fight or struggle. All was going well, considering.

However, as they rounded the corner and turned into the little gate of their house, Gemma gasped. Griswold was on the porch, unlocking the front door.

Chapter Twelve

Griswold, in the act of pushing the door open, froze. "What the...?" His face paled to a sickly grey as he stared at the scene before him.

"*...if I had known for just a second you'd be back to bother me. Go on now—hic—go! Walk out the door. Jus' turn around 'cos you're not welcome...*" Beryl warbled, punctuating the lines by stabbing the rose in the air.

Oswin and Gemma, having pushed the wheelbarrow as far as the door, stopped and silently, gently let it down and stepped back. Griswold, eyes wide and staring, moved to it, slowly leaned down until his nose was almost touching Beryl's.

"You're *drunk!*" he snapped.

She blinked at him hazily.

After a moment's hesitation, Beryl said, "Father! I have an announcement to make. I think I'm over him now. It's been tough. But I think I'll survive without his love. *Yes, I will survive, just as long as I...*"

As she slipped into her song once more, the curtains down the street fluttered into action as faces peeked out.

"Oh, for crying out loud! Let's get her upstairs to bed," Griswold said. He was barely audible above Beryl's singing as he hoisted her up out of the wheelbarrow. "You two haven't been drinking have you? Let me smell your breath."

There was an ominous hush as Beryl went quiet for a moment.

"Oh no! Oh no! I'm going to be sick! To the loo! To the loo!" she boomed to all the neighbors, before leaping free of Griswold, running through the door and bounding up the stairs two at a time, with the eerie speed and purpose of a dolphin torpedoing through the water, leaving the rest staring agog at her disappearing bulk.

She was lavishly sick for ten whole minutes, during which time she called repeatedly for her back to be patted. Then, demanding an escort to literally hold her hand, although she was on all fours, she took a further ten minutes to crawl, groaning, across the landing to her room. There she insisted on being hoisted into bed, and on having Gemma mop her face with a damp cloth until she fell asleep.

* * * *

The next morning Griswold replaced the curtain rails in Beryl's room, as she groaned and tossed in her bed. She called for Gemma to mop her brow again.

Gemma sat with the cloth limp in her lap, her mobile phone in her hands, staring open mouthed at the foot of Beryl's bed. Her heart pounded so fast she should be running, but she knew her legs were too jellied up with fear to carry her and her stomach was a churning pit of terror. For there at the foot of Beryl's bed was the ghost.

The ghost stood in her housecoat and her scarf with curlers on her head. Her arms were folded in front of her, and she unfolded them regularly to bring a cigarette to her lips. All the while staring at Beryl. She wore a readable expression today—a mixture of contempt and disgust. But there was more. In the smoke meandering lazily from her cigarette, were two little shapes. As light and gaseous as the smoke themselves, they writhed and twisted in a playful dance in the illusive substance.

Griswold was plainly unaware of the visitors and busy muttering to himself about Beryl's shameful lapse into drunkenness. Beryl, of course, was also insensitive to the ghosts. She took Gemma's hand and whispered feebly, "Gemma tell me...ooh, my head!—it hurts *so*...to speak, but I must ask...it didn't happen...just an awful nightmare...my Coast sweater in the toilet...it was just a dream, wasn't it?" There was a pause as Gemma gazed wide-eyed at the foot of the bed. Beryl mustered all her strength. "Wasn't it? *Ooh, my head!*"

"Yes Beryl," Gemma mumbled in flat, dead tones and without turning to face Beryl. "It was all just a horrible dream."

Her fingers had been so unsteady, her text had come out badly, but Oswin had read it and understood at once.

"Ghost Bs rm now."

He snatched up the Ghost-O-Meter and skidded across the hall. There he saw where Gemma, eyes like saucers and deathly pale, stared transfixed at the foot of Beryl's bed. Her stupid family had not the slightest inkling that Gemma was in a state of absolute terror. Oswin's detector sprang into life before he had aimed it properly at the foot of the bed.

Its LCD indicator lights flashed and it clicked and whistled gaily and loudly.

"Wwheeeee...click...click...pop...wwwwheeeeeeeeeeeeuuuuu..."

went the ghost detector.

Oswin's grinned wide. It was working perfectly. The atmosphere at the foot of Beryl's bed was indeed highly charged. And the room was cold. Whatever it was that Gemma was seeing—for Oswin could see nothing—was there in a field of highly active particles at least. And it was a biggie.

At the noise of the detector, Beryl let out a long, shivering moan and pulled the quilt over her head. "*Noooooo!*"

Griswold, who was standing on a chair by the window, spun around. He wobbled dangerously on his platform.

"*Oi!* Quit it!" he snarled, but in his heart of hearts he thought it was good to see his nephew sporting a toy gun—a real boy's toy. What a refreshing change from all that swatting and tinkering with test tubes!

Besides, it was just desserts for Beryl to have her hangover worsened by that awful racket! He smiled. Griswold's smiles consisted of a quick flash of teeth behind his bristling moustache; they were easily missed as they faded instantly.

"Bloody kids!" he muttered, turning back to his work.

Gemma blinked, shivered and rubbed her face. Then she turned to Oswin. "It's gone," she mouthed. "Did you see it?"

Oswin shook his head. He took another reading instantly—Griswold wobbled, Beryl moaned—and it was ever so slightly lower. Almost too good to be true!

Oswin came in every ten minutes for an hour and took readings. The audio indicator grew quieter with each reading and the lights display, fainter and briefer. But Beryl's protesting wails did not.

"Aw, now look, boy," Griswold said at last. "You've run the battery down already!"

Oswin looked at him for a moment before saying, "Er...yeah, well, at least it's not so loud now."

Gemma took a page and a half to describe the sighting in her diary and dutifully recorded the readings.

"I hope you don't mind, Gemma, but I'll be handing in your ghost diary to my teacher as part of the project. You're like a subject in my project."

"Yeah, I know," she said absently, as she sketched what she had seen with remarkable ease and accuracy.

"I never knew you could draw," Oswin remarked, looking over her shoulder. "That's really good! Looks quite spooky, though."

"It was. I don't like those little things!" Gemma shuddered. "I used to assume it was all one ghost, but now I know they're not the housewife ghost. And she doesn't seem so frightening to me now."

"How do you feel about being the only one who saw them, though?" Oswin asked. He wasn't merely curious; he needed the data for his project. Without proper scientific back up and psychological analysis, it would all be a load of prattling nonsense in his teacher's eyes.

"It makes me feel kind of...insane," Gemma said quietly.

"Well, you're not! We've got proof that you saw something." Oswin patted the detector. "We've got proof! You're creative and imaginative and wonderful. But you're not crazy. Don't let anyone tell you you're mad!"

In the pause that followed, Gemma continued drawing quietly.

"I was thinking that you may be psychic, though," Oswin said. "Psychic people probably have some quality that makes them able to see these charged fields. It's like a gift, Gem, like your dancing. You're gifted."

Chapter Thirteen

Things were quiet for a few days. Griswold was home a lot more than usual. It was the football finals and he had arranged his work schedule so that he could watch as many games as possible. Beryl had stocked him up with enough of his favorite brand of lager and snacks to keep him happy whilst riveted to his favorite telly chair. Having no sensitivity to paranormal activity, she sat in the chair next to his—the housewife ghost's favorite chair—and watched a bit of the game with him. This meant Gemma was left alone more than usual and life was generally calmer in the house.

In fact, the house was filled with an air of optimism. Not only was Griswold happier because he was watching the game, but the girls knew this and made use of his relaxed pre-occupation to ask requests of him. Things like, *'Can I have a bit of extra pocket money to get those new shoes?'* and *'Is this skirt too short to wear down to my mate's house? Thought not.'* And *'Can I go to that fancy dress party, then?'*

Gemma chose her timing down to the last second. She waited outside the door until she heard the adverts come on. Father hardly had time to ask Beryl to get him another can of beer when Gemma pushed the door open and appeared like a superhero answering a distress call, with a fresh lager in her hand and a top-up of Bombay mix.

"Daddy, you never gave me a straight answer about...about... *Oswin!*" She faltered, because she was looking at Beryl sitting on the housewife ghost, who was knitting her dull sweater from behind Beryl's bulk. Beryl herself was shelling pistachios and popping them gracefully into her mouth. So she looked both fuddy duddy and exotically elegant at once. And alarmingly strange with two pairs of arms working independently. Gemma felt a rush of amusement and fear both at once. She fought to quell her emotions, as she continued.

"...*Oswin!*...about the fancy dress party. It's in a Church hall. Everyone going is in my age group. So can I go?" She gabbled her request out and rushed to the door to call again for Oswin, before turning back to hear Griswold's reply.

"Hmm? What party is this then? What about Oswin?" asked

her father blearily; it was hard for him to switch his brain from football to girls' parties so quickly. And Gemma's dancing about didn't help his confusion.

"Nothing about Oswin. Stop calling Oswin, Gemma, you'll only confuse Father," Beryl interrupted then turned to Griswold and spoke loudly and slowly. "It's Rebecca Wilson's birthday party; she wants to go to it."

Beryl held a pistachio daintily poised to be popped in her mouth as soon as she had finished talking, the ghost's pair of hands knitting rhythmically all the time. "She's been asking about it for ages. It's the one she wants to go to, dressed as that *Shrek* character. All green."

"Who—Rebecca?" frowned Griswold.

"No. Our Gemma. It's all properly chaperoned. Let her go!" She winked exuberantly at Gemma and grinned.

"Well, all right, I suppose so," Griswold grumbled, "if it's properly chaperoned. What time does it end?"

But right then the advertisements ended and his attention was taken.

Oswin, having heard Gemma's distressed call, knew by the tone what it meant and came bounding down the stairs with his detector at the ready. He alone noticed Gemma point at Beryl and, coming round the back of the chairs, aimed at Beryl and pulled the trigger. He couldn't see the ghost, and therefore didn't know that, with a fleeting look of annoyance, she had vanished upon his entrance.

"*Wheeeeeeee click click click...*" went the detector.

"*Oi!*" yelled Griswold.

"I beg your pardon!" Beryl gasped, bristling angrily. "It is extremely rude and aggressive—so much so in fact, that it is illegal to..."

"*Oi!* I'm trying to watch the game! Shut it or get out. *Now!* The pair of you."

Oswin, having taken a reading, muttered an apology as he scampered out at once. Beryl opened and shut her mouth before shaking her head in tearful indignation and turning back to the telly.

By the end of the game Beryl was livid. She cornered Oswin and Gemma and had strong and lengthy words with the pair of them.

"I don't appreciate this blatant attack on my person by you two," she said as she served them a warmed-up pizza for their tea. It was dry and burnt along the edges and they suspected that Beryl was glad it had turned out like that. "How do you think I felt, being targeted in that way? It was a sinister attack. I felt like an IRA victim. You took turns continually to shoot me in the back of the head with that stupid toy gun that Oswin's taken to carrying about. Oh, and it looks disturbingly childish, by the way! Sorry, but I feel I have to tell you that. It's getting too late for you to suddenly start enjoying your childhood!"

"I thought I'd give being a proper child a go before I reached puberty," he replied as he bit into his slice of pizza. Beryl and Griswold had always gone on about him being unnaturally mature.

Gemma almost choked on a piece of pizza and kicked him from under the table.

"It's not like it seems," she said when she recovered from her coughing fit. "It's a...it's like a test. For Oswin's project. He had to take certain measurements."

Oswin was unable to speak for himself just then, as he was battling to get a bit of crust ground down enough to be swallowed.

Beryl harped on. "And you only got away with victimizing me because Father was so engrossed in the game. You were clever enough to turn down the sound of the gun as you went along with your prolonged and vicious attack."

"Beryl, please! It's not like that at all," Gemma said.

But there was no placating Beryl. "I know what this is about," she said with tearful bitterness as she plonked herself down at the kitchen table. "It's because of Raj. Because I'm seeing a bloke from the arts block, isn't it—someone who isn't academic enough for the likes of you?"

Gemma and Oswin stared for a moment. Beryl took a mighty bite out of a slice of pizza and chewed like a weepy camel working on a piece of cud.

They had no idea Beryl had a boyfriend. When did this happen? Just then the tap at the sink opened up, and let out sorry dribble of water with gulping sounds. Quick as gun-slinger, Oswin whipped out the Ghost-O-Meter, aimed, and fired.

"*Click, click, phut...*" It indicated nothing.

But just then, Gemma screamed, convinced of a scuttling movement across the table. A feeling of malice swept over her like a gust of wind and she found herself inexplicably gulping down tears. There was a clunk on the table. Someone—something— knocked over the pepper grinder. And Oswin aimed at the table.

"*Wheeeeeeeeeee click click click pop!*"

Beryl jumped, almost choked, and rose up with bulging eyes.

"Right! That's it!" she yelled, her face flushing to puce. "I am not sitting at the table with the pair of you!" She grabbed what was left of the communal pizza and marched off to her bedroom.

There was a moment's silence. Griswold who had been asleep—full of Bombay mix, lager and footie—in his chair in the front room, stirred and coughed. Then all was still again. Gemma sniffed and wiped her eyes.

"You got quite a fright," Oswin said quietly.

"I thought I saw something out of the corner of my eye," Gemma whispered. Her face was pale. "Something lunging at me, filled with hatred and...malice! Yes, malice, like it would destroy me if it could. It was—creepy. Do you ever get that?"

"No, not really," Oswin said, "apart from Beryl. But the ghost meter says it wasn't all in your head. Unlike the dripping tap, which *I* thought was something." He grinned ruefully. "Trouble is with this other *entity* is that it's so difficult to detect properly. I mean, with the ghost, when she's there—there she is! You see her. Whereas with this sort of thing, it could be just normal knocks and bumps that are genuinely explained away, or it could be something else, at any given time."

"You mean, this sort of thing comes and goes without being noticed, more than we realize?"

"Exactly! And it does things—moves objects, and breaks stuff...shoves pink sweaters in the loo."

"That's true! And the only time I've had a good look at it, was when there was a pair of them. They were playing in the cigarette smoke of the old housewife ghost. Not worrying any of us in particular. Just...playing." Gemma paused a while before asking, "Do you...do you think they're fairies?"

Oswin shrugged and scraped his fingers through his hair. "Possibly. But the angle I'm going to concentrate on in my project is that whatever they are, their little tricks are not as sweet and innocent as they may seem. Like you felt—they may be malignant."

Gemma could not disagree with that and they both decided to be extra vigilant about things falling over and of other phenomena, such as burning smells.

So that was why, when a few days later, they both rushed around the house in a bit of a panic.

Chapter Fourteen

"I can smell burning! Can you smell burning?" Gemma gabbled, bumping into Oswin on the landing.

"Yeah! What can it be?"

"It's definitely not downstairs." Gemma sniffed frantically. "I've checked all around downstairs."

Sniffing, they moved upstairs, following the sent like a pair of bloodhounds.

"It's coming from Beryl's room!" Gemma exclaimed, stopping suddenly. She was beginning to feel a tad dizzy with all the sniffing.

Oswin, crinkling his nose, paused and nodded. They tapped on the door.

"Beryl?" enquired Gemma quietly then louder, more urgently. "Beryl are you alright?"

There was a sigh and an irritable tut, audible from outside the closed door.

"Come!" Beryl called haughtily. But they were already bursting in.

She sat amid her usual tumble of books and files, frowning up at them from the floor. "Yes? What is it?"

"Oh!" Gemma faltered. "I...we thought we smelled something burning."

"Well, actually you did." Beryl pointed to a newly bought incense burner, with a joss stick burning on it.

"Ah, I see!" Oswin said. "What fragrance? Nag Champa?"

Gemma stared at the smoke twirling up and writhing around the room.

"It's to help me concentrate, in my studying," Beryl said defensively. "The woman at the shop told me about it. It's authentic. Us British don't make proper use of all the elements of aromatherapy around us."

Oswin watched Gemma's eyes flitting as she watched the twisting smoke. Her pupils were wide and her mouth set in a rigid line of fear.

"Right," he said absently.

"There's nothing wrong with adopting a new and artistic way

of thinking. The new age sciences have so much to offer..." Beryl prattled on in a dreamy manner.

"Right," Oswin, said reaching slowly for his belt. "I'm just going to take a little shot at the smoke."

"Wheeeeeeeeeeee click, click, click pop!" screeched the Ghost-O-Meter, followed by a shocked pause.

"That is not funny!" Beryl cried. "Just because he's a performing art student, you think you've got to tease me about it! He can't help it if he's not academically inclined! He's clever in his own, creative way!"

"No, I wasn't teasing you! I just had to take a shot at the smoke... er...boys stuff...you know?" Oswin smiled lamely and shunted his specs up the bridge of his nose.

Beryl's eyes narrowed, "I know what this is all about. I know what all this shooting at things of mine and at me—at the back of my head—is all about! It's because of Raj, isn't it? Just because he's not academic?"

"No, honest," said Gemma turning to face the others. "It's nice about you and Raj, honest."

"Nice?" Beryl spat with mocking disbelief. "Nice? Huh! It's a free country do you hear? I'll go out with whomever I bloody well want to. Nothing is going to tear Raj and I apart—nothing! Now get out! I'm studying. Just because I am in a serious and committed relationship with a boy from the performing arts block, doesn't meant that my studies are going to suffer. You'll see! Now, leave me alone. Go on!"

There was no telling Beryl; Gemma and Oswin departed meekly. In any case they were itching to discuss issues more interesting to them than who Beryl was dating at present.

For Beryl's part, left to dream and study simultaneously, this was the most exciting romance she had ever embarked on. Raj was artistic, not studious and the knowledge that his parents disapproved of his playing bass guitar in a friend's garage on Saturdays, was an added bonus. Watching his rebellion was exhilarating and at little risk to herself. She stopped chewing her way through the classic novels and began to read urban fantasy paperbacks instead. She painted her nails black and borrowed some of his secret stash of Bizarre Magazines and had a go at writing lyrics for his tunes. Once she had spent a few afternoons visiting Raj at his home, she even began to try out Indian cuisine—the eating of it, that is, not the tedious cooking—and burnt incense in her room when Father was about and all around the house when he was out.

Griswold played his role perfectly; he did not approve, especially when he learnt that Raj and his friends had formed a band that practised in a garage. And he was convinced that by burning incense, Beryl was disguising the smell of something more sinister, like cigarette smoke or—worse—cannabis.

Which is why Oswin, coming down for a cup of juice one evening, saw Griswold rummaging through the dust bin in the kitchen. Straightening up, red-faced, Griswold explained himself.

"Aha! Ashes!" he cried and beckoned to Oswin. "Look here boy, there are ashes in this bin and a sweet smell lingering in the air. I work my butt off to provide for these girls and this is how they repay me. By turning to drugs while I'm out slaving away for their futures."

Oswin examined the ashes. "Actually, that's long and thin. And see the strands of fibres left? That's Beryl's incense stick she was burning. She said the kitchen smelled funny."

Griswold grunted, looking about with narrowed eyes. "Hmph! Well it does now!" He sniffed the air.

Oswin pointed to the packaging in the bin. "It was those samosas she heated up for our tea."

"Hmm..." Griswold continued to scan the room. "The only reason for burning joss sticks in my day was to hide the sickly smell of cannabis!"

Oswin grinned. "Nah! Your Beryl is very straight, really. Outrageous but square. Besides, it's because of her boyfriend, isn't it?"

"What boyfriend?"

"She...er...likes this bloke. And he's into a bit of Gothic pop and incense, so *she*'s going for it too." He shrugged trying to look as casual as he could. "That's why she's wearing that dreadful purple lipstick lately. Just a passing phase, really."

"Excuse me!" Beryl boomed from the doorway. "Do you two mind telling me why are you men rummaging through the kitchen bin like a pair of homeless veterans outside McDonald's?"

Oswin and Griswold jumped and both sprang to shut the bin lid. In the process it was knocked over and the day's garbage spilled across the floor. Beryl stood over them in great disapproval as, on their hands and knees, they gathered up the trash.

"Hey, look at this!" gasped Oswin. He picked something small out of the strands of Gemma's uneaten spaghetti.

"That's mine!" Beryl cried, stepping forward to snatch it from Oswin's grasp. "What's it doing in the bin? Who threw my skull ring into the bin?"

Neither Griswold nor Oswin could answer her question.

"I want to know who did this," she declared, looking about the room, as though expecting an answer. "This is a personal attack on me—throwing my skull ring into the bin! It's proper silver and all!"

"Perhaps it got there by accident," Oswin suggested at last.

"I took it off to wash the pots and..."

"Well, it could have ended up under a pile of cartons and into the bin," Griswold suggested. But Beryl was not convinced.

"Excuse me! I'll have you know that I am always far too careful with my jewelry to accidentally leave it lying about to be thrown away with the garbage. Not *me*. I always hang it on the tea towel peg," she insisted. "There's no *way* it could end up in the bin."

An idea struck Oswin, "Let me shoot it for you," he said.

"Don't be daft, boy!" Griswold hissed, but his warning was too late. The gun gave a feeble wheeze and crackle before dying. Beryl stood gaping at Oswin.

"Hmm. Not a *bad* reading," he muttered to himself. "But nothing conclusive."

"How dare you! Father, do you see how he's always shooting at me lately?"

"Now, don't be paranoid, pet! The boy shoots at any old thing."

Just then Gemma trailed in, practising a dance routine, "...two, three..s-l-i-d-e...ta...ta...one...uh, hello!...three...s-l-i-d-e..." she stopped dead and gasped then retreated very quickly, still dancing.

Oswin looked from Gemma to where she'd been looking when she gasped. He aimed and fired.

"*Wheeeeeeee...click...click...click...pop!*"

"There, see?" said Griswold. "The boy shoots at anything and everything."

"This is not fair!" Beryl said as she stormed off to the front room. "I am being persecuted and no one notices!"

Griswold stared after her and sighed. "Well, clean this mess up, boy! What's on telly tonight? That's what I want, to relax in front of the box and unwind after a hard day's work. Not come home to all this madness!"

He continued to complain as Oswin picked up the remaining rubbish and swept the floor with a brush and dustpan. "I can't believe some of the things I come home to! Beryl with a boyfriend from some 'block' she keeps ranting about. Did you see him? He wears eye liner and buys her biker rings! And now she's burning camouflaging scents and ranting and raving like a loony. And Gemma prancing around in a dreamlike state, painting herself all colors of the rainbow. Did you see the glazed look on her face, boy?" Griswold hissed. "I worry about these girls, boy, I really worry."

"Gemma's always been a bit dreamy," Oswin said, fetching the dust pan and brush from the broom cupboard. "And Beryl..."

"Father!" Beryl called from the front room, "that reality program you like is on now!"

Griswold's face lit up. "Now that's what *I'd* like, boy!" he said, making for the door. "Spy cameras planted all through the house. Then I could keep a proper eye on these girls of mine."

"Well, it's easily done," Oswin replied absently. "I doubt it would cost too much either."

Griswold whipped round and gawped. "Really?"

"Father!"

"Yeah," Oswin assured him. "I could set a few up in a couple of days. I know where to get them and all. A boy in my class is doing a project with..."

"Father!"

Griswold glanced over his shoulder distractedly. "Alright, alright, I'm coming!" He turned back to Oswin with a gleam in his eye and whispered, "tell you what, son, I'll give you a cheque. You set it all up for me!" He rubbed his hands together and chuckled as he turned to go. Then he turned back. "Oh, and boy," he said, "fetch me a nice cup of hot chocolate and a couple of biscuits into the front room will you? There's a lad!" And he winked at Oswin before trotting off to watch his program.

Oswin shook his head, checked his watch and aimed his gun again. He had to go by memory, because he had been unable to see what Gemma had seen. Then he stopped. A slow smile spread across his face.

"Yes!" He punched the air. "Brilliant! Thank you, uncle Griswold!" Oswin chuckled to himself as he put the kettle on. "Thank you and all!"

Chapter Fifteen

After the weekend, when he'd come back from visiting home, Oswin glanced at Gemma's latest recording in her ghost diary and confirmed that they matched his plotted readings.

"When do you have to hand this in?" Gemma asked. "Would you like me to take the pretty cover off?"

"It's due in at the end of term. I guess it can stay the way it is. The important thing is how nicely the sightings match up with the readings."

"It's a pity it's only me who sees anything," she sighed.

Oswin smiled as he pulled out his notes on his unsuccessful headgear, "That may change," he said. "I have Griswold's...er... backing to install a few camera's around the house."

"Really? But I thought..."

"More important, is what he thinks. He's asked me to put up surveillance cameras..."

"Why?" asked Gemma.

Oswin told her about Griswold's worries that Beryl was smoking cannabis. At that they both sniggered before he continued. "He thinks if the house is rigged up like a TV reality programme, he'll feel more at ease. Spying on you girls, and me too, I suppose."

"Can you imagine what Beryl will say when she finds out?" Gemma gasped and covered her mouth with her hands.

"I shudder to think!"

In less than two weeks the cameras were installed. Oswin set two in the bedrooms, the kitchen, the front room, the entrance and the landing. One was to take normal footage and the other had been adapted to show heat and magnetic abnormalities in the air—ghosts. And he hadn't had to foot the bill. Both the cameras in the girls' rooms were rigged to come on only when there was a change in the air and he had been sorely tempted to make sure the normal cameras were permanently out of order.

So, as it is with these things, once everything was nicely set up to visually record the haunting, there was a lull in paranormal activity. Even the housewife ghost refused to come out.

"Isn't this frustrating!" Oswin growled as he surveyed the scant recordings in Gemma's diary. "For the first few days there was nothing. Absolutely nothing. Now Beryl lights one of her stink sticks up and the cameras go on, but there's no ghostly movement at all."

Gemma was lying on his bed again, tapping a dance routine out on the wall. It was the sort of dance that used plenty of airy-fairy movements on the arms and she incorporated these as best she could.

"So the normal camera's filming right now?" she asked, sitting up.

Oswin nodded.

"What's she doing?"

He glanced sulkily at the monitor, before replying, "sitting on the floor shuffling papers."

Gemma moved to stare at the screens. One was blank and the other showed Beryl settling down to do some studying.

"How can she study all over the floor like that?" Oswin remarked. "You'd think she'd go down to the kitchen,"

"She likes her privacy, like *Shrek*," Gemma replied with a giggle.

Oswin felt a pang of guilt.

"Why don't I go in and see if I can see anything?" Gemma asked. "I'll say I'm making coffee and does she want some?"

"Okay, go on then!"

When Gemma returned moments later, it was to say she had seen nothing unusual.

"They know we're watching them," Oswin said. "Ghosts do this to you every time. They just *won't* be captured on film."

"Well, if the ghosts are hiding away from the cameras, why don't we just switch them off for a few days? That way we might entice some sort of appearance."

With a nod, Oswin decided to do just that.

* * * *

Someone else was very aware of the cameras. Griswold would come home, throw his briefcase and jacket in a slothful heap in the entrance, only to remember the cameras and return to hang his jacket and put his case away diligently. Or when he was scoffing down his TV supper, he would suddenly remember his manners and sit up straight and eat more slowly. He was so embarrassed when he fell asleep in his chair, drooling a little as he snored, that he rushed up to Oswin's room to demand that he remove that footage immediately.

"Oh...er...I...er..." Oswin spluttered, thinking fast. "I switched it off when you came in the room. I thought..."

"Good lad!" Griswold cried. "No need to include me in it, eh? By the way, have you got any interesting stuff on the girls yet?"

"Sorry, no. Just Beryl burning her incense while studying a few times. Definitely nothing to worry about."

"Hmm." Griswold was still unconvinced. "Well, keep filming for another week or so. Then I'll have a look at your most interesting shots."

"Right," Oswin replied casually, but when Griswold left his room, he rubbed his forehead vigorously. Darn! He hadn't thought of that—having to produce videos! Still it was easily solved.

He set the cameras to film breakfast time—such as it was—a bit of afternoon time in the front room and in the hall and landing, for reality's sake. And a snippet of time in the girls' rooms, when he least expected them to be dressing or picking their noses. The next thing was—should he warn them? He decided that in order to get natural behavior from them, it would be best not to say anything. It was bad enough having Griswold minding his Ps and Qs in an exaggerated way. All that straight backed posture made him look like he had a spinal injury. It was a wonder Beryl hadn't picked up on his behavior and asked questions.

Needless to say, nothing interesting happened—either in terms of paranormal activity, or anything worthwhile to send in to You've Been Framed. Oswin was beginning to loose hope. Gemma's ghost diary was certainly not scientific enough to be used for his project alone. His teacher would probably think it was a fabrication. Unless his detecting equipment got enough testing, his project was doomed to failure. He was now using his weekends at home to work on a more earthly-based project—a working, mechanical pair of grasshopper legs. Although he had hardly any time left to do it justice and get a good mark, at least he would have something concrete to hand in. He could feel a *'long talk'* with his parents looming and was beginning to spend more time thinking about his grasshopper leg project than his ghost hunt. In fact, he had quite forgotten about the cameras waiting to film the resident ghosts when the next event finally happened.

They were, strangely enough, all at the kitchen table at the same time. It was Saturday morning and Oswin was waiting for his parents to collect him. Griswold had just come in from fetching his paper, bringing hot croissants from the bakery and this had lured everyone to the kitchen. The girls were still in their gowns but Oswin was fully dressed, eager to get home to work on his new project. At the sound of a passing car he turned to look through the kitchen doorway and down the short passage to the front door.

"Is your mother coming this morning, then?" Griswold asked.

Oswin nodded and said, "She's not working today, so I asked her to come as soon as she could."

"I'll tell her to stop by for dinner just as soon as Beryl is over this incense burning faze," Griswold said, giving her a pointed stare. "We don't want your parents to think this is a Sixties, hippie commune we live in."

Beryl spluttered, struggling to swallow a mouthful of pastry and jam. "I beg your pardon! Excuse my precocity, but I'll have you know, Father, that I burn incense sticks as part of an aromatherapy program. Aromatherapy is used to enhance one's sense of well-being and to either relax, or invigorate one..."

"I was only pointing out that it looks..."

"Excuse me," Beryl pushed her way back into the speakers chair with studied ease. "Let me finish what I am saying, before you interrupt me, please. It's only fair!"

"But..."

"I am trying to improve my vitality levels to aid me in the forthcoming exams," she continued. "This has nothing to do with the nineteen sixties drug culture—something I am sure *you* were involved in, in some level or the other. *I*, however, am not that way inclined, thank you very much! I am simply trying to do well in my exams. For it is not only *gifted* pupils that put effort into their schooling, but it is also the more average scholar who tries hard—if not harder—than those labelled talented. Now, in my extreme efforts—which obviously go unappreciated—to do well in my exams and get as good a mark as I can and at the same time to continue unabated in my nurturing role as Mother of the House, I feel I should be allowed to employ natural and *harmless* methods of enhancing my efforts. I take great offence at your suspicious insinuations..."

By now, Griswold and Oswin had glazed over and were staring dismally into middle space and Gemma had shut her eyes in an effort to escape the intense volley of defence from Beryl. Only the salt cellar tumbling over jolted everyone back to the here and now.

"Oh, look what you've done," Griswold snapped, as the tall and unstable container clattered onto a plate. "Be careful, Beryl!"

The salt cellar had crashed down onto Beryl's marmalade croissant and somehow the plug at the back came out. Now a heap of salt lay accusingly amongst the breakfast clutter, and the holes of the salt cellar were blocked up by a blob of marmalade.

"I never touched the darn thing!" Beryl cried indignantly. "I was nowhere near it."

Oswin pricked his ears up at once. He glanced at the clock, at Beryl and the toppled salt cellar, back at the clock, and gave Gemma a pointed look. She shrugged.

At first, Beryl and Griswold were too busy arguing to notice this interaction.

"I was not waving my arms about!" Beryl declared. "Nothing of the sort!"

"Now, Beryl..." Griswold tried to get a word in edgeways, but she cut him off with all the efficiency of a Wilkinson's sword.

"I may have gesticulated what I was saying, but I had no choice! I was speaking in defence against unfair accusations, which made me slightly emotional, but...let me finish!...but I was not waving my arms about wildly. I've been having marmalade...excuse me Father, don't look away! I am going to finish what I have to say... I've been eating marmalade and croissants, so why would I have the salt cellar handy? It was, you must admit in all fairness, not that close...Oswin, what are you *doing?*"

Oswin was trying to measure the position the salt cellar was in before it toppled and the direction in which it fell, in order to get a good idea of where the force that pushed it over came from. He had his own theories about who—or what—was responsible for knocking it over.

"We just want to clear up the spilt salt," Gemma said peaceably.

"I want Beryl to do that!" Griswold snapped, "as she was the one..."

"How dare you! I have spent ages and ages calmly putting my defence forward and you don't even acknowledge the fact that I have!" Losing her courtroom calm, Beryl took to thumping the table and yelling, "It's all because I have a relationship with someone from the performing arts block!"

"Enough!" Griswold roared.

Everyone jumped. Beryl, who had begun to scrape back her chair in order to make a dramatic and tearful exit as she spoke, froze, sitting still on her chair, a hand to her mouth, her chair positioned away from the table. All was still and silent for a moment. That's when they heard it.

Chapter Sixteen

They all heard someone at the door. The shuffle, stamp and click that proceeds the chink of keys or the ring of the bell. Just a little noise—a routine lasting little more than a second—they had all heard often enough to recognise instantly. It was a sound that could drift down the hall and easily be heard in the kitchen-diner if the doors were open, and if everyone in the room were being particularly quiet. Had it occurred a moment earlier, they would have been none the wiser. But they all heard the sound and calmed down instantly to receive their guest.

Griswold shut his eyes. "That would be your mum, Oswin. Let her in," he said quietly.

Oswin went at once and quickly, barely noticing a flutter of movement in the front room doorway as he passed. But as he got to the front door, opening it, he saw no one was there. He realized with a start the doorbell had not rung yet. It should have rung before he'd left the kitchen diner—as he pushed his chair back, even. Only then did he take in the movement he had seen out of the corner of his eye by the front room door. He rushed back, heart racing, to that door. All was lifeless. He crept into the room, thinking *Is it an intruder?* No. Nothing. There was nobody there at all.

"Isn't she come yet?" The question rang clear and suddenly through the air.

Oswin gasped with fright as he spun around. "Gosh, Gemma, you didn't half give me a start!" he whispered.

She stared at him for a moment then her eyes scanned the room.

"Quick—where's the ghost meter?" Oswin said. "Oh, why did I stop carrying it around with me? Oh, where did I put it?"

At this point Griswold came into the room. "Where is she, then?" he asked.

"No. It's no one," Oswin replied. "It must have been...our imagination."

"Well, never mind, boy," Griswold said kindly, as he turned to go back to the kitchen. "She'll be along soon. Any minute now."

Recalling that his meter was on his desk, Oswin made for the stairs. He only vaguely heard the doorbell ring as he fumbled amongst various papers and paraphernalia. As he tore back down, taking the stairs two at a time, his mother, Martha, opened her arms to greet him.

"My!" she gasped, "I hope you haven't been missing home that much!"

"He seems very happy here, Martha," Griswold insisted, eyeing them warily.

Wheeeeeeee...click...click...click...pop! went the gun as Oswin, still in his mother's embrace, fired it at the front door.

"Oh!" She jumped and involuntarily let him go. He spun round and bounded to the front room door and fired. *Wheeeeeeee...click...click...click...pop!*

"Full count!" he chuckled and strode to the kitchen-diner and Gemma nodded, scribbling furiously in her diary.

Griswold grinned helplessly at Martha. "Er...see? Happy as a lark, he's been. I thought his phase of playing with that gun was over, but apparently not! Perhaps he's brought it out to show you. I believe he built it himself!"

"Ah, yes, well...I'm sure he's happy here—as always, Griswold," she replied above a '*Wheeeeeeee...click...click...click...pip!*' coming from the kitchen.

"Only two notches down! Not bad considering the time delay!" Oswin called.

Griswold and Martha smiled indulgently at each other. However, they froze in their polite stances as they heard Beryl roaring from the kitchen, "You little.....!" This was interrupted by a crash! A bang! And scrapings ensued, punctuated by the strangled cries of the cousins struggling.

The adults ran towards the commotion and found Beryl and Oswin wrestling furiously over his space gun.

"Beryl!" cried Griswold. "Leave the boy...*Beryl!*" He pried the pair apart manually as he continued, "Don't bully! He's much smaller than you!"

"I won't have him shooting at me! I won't tolerate such abuse!" screeched Beryl, red faced and panting.

"Oswin," reproached his mother, "don't tease the girls! He doesn't tease the girls does he, Griswold?"

"No!" Griswold's voice was strained by his exertion as he held Beryl at an arm's length from the Oswin and his gun.

"Oh yes he does!" Beryl said heatedly. "All the time!"

"No, he doesn't Martha, I can assure..."

"I'm going to break that gun now!" Beryl yelled. Arteries

swelled out on her neck and her eyes bulged.

"Don't you dare! It's an important..." Oswin snapped, his eyes flashing like cold steel. But he didn't finish. Beryl tore herself free from her father's restraint and made for the door.

"You're all targeting me! Victimizing me, just because I've got a boyfriend on the arts block! He may only be on the performing arts course, but he's a sensitive and creative boyfriend, who's clever in his own way!"

Sobbing, she brushed passed Martha and scaled the stairs, stepping over Gemma on the way. Gemma was huddled at the bottom of the stairs, still writing furiously in her diary. Her aunt glanced at her and at Beryl disappearing up the stairs. Within seconds, Beryl's romantic weeping could be heard drifting gently down the stairs, for she had left her bedroom door open. Martha stared up the stairs for a moment before turning back to Griswold.

He squirmed. "Er...our Gemma's taken to writing a journal."

"That's nice! Look, why don't you put the kettle on and make a cup of tea for us?" she said kindly. "Teenagers! I'll go and have a little chat with your Beryl, if you like. Woman to woman—would that be of help to you? I don't want to interfere, but if that would be useful...?"

Griswold blushed deeply and coughed, "Er...yes, thank you Martha. Perhaps she's missing her mother at the minute. Exams looming and what not. She's fine, usually. This is not an example of what it's normally like here..."

"I know, I know. Don't worry yourself, pet," Martha said indulgently, squeezing his wrist briefly. "You're doing a fine job with your girls. A fine job!"

Thanks to his mother's staying for soothing cups of tea and girlie heart to hearts, Oswin was able to take a full hour's worth of readings. And he puffed out with happiness to note that they came down steadily, as predicted, from their higher reading.

Martha told him off for repeatedly setting the noisy gun off. "Oswin, please! It's nice that you can play imaginative games, but for pity's sake—have some sensitivity!"

"Never mind, Martha," Griswold grinned, glad to reverse rolls and support her in *her* embarrassment. "As you can hear, the battery is running down. Again."

The adults assumed he'd lost interest in his game when the intermittent firing stopped altogether. In fact, Oswin *had* forgotten to take the last two readings, because he had gone up to his room to look at the breakfast time footage—and found something very interesting.

Gemma started to clear up the breakfast things and pack the dishwasher but she left the task half way through to run up after Oswin and peek round his bedroom door. He had been scanning the surveillance footage for that morning.

His face beamed back at her, aglow with success.

"Two things," he said in a choked voice, as he pressed the re-play button to show her. "All this time—nothing! And now *two things in one go!*"

"Things always happen in threes," Gemma murmured but if Oswin heard he didn't acknowledge her comment.

"The salt cellar. Look!" He beamed.

Gemma strained to view the footage. It was somewhat blurred and in black and white, but it was clearing the earlier breakfast scene. Then she gasped. Sure enough in the ghost sensitive camera, a little white blob could clearly be seen darting from the clock to the table. It sprang up at the salt cellar—which, like everything else was mostly blurred shades of grey—and knocked it down before bounding off the table and disappearing off camera.

"And look here!" Oswin's hands trembled as he switched to the footage of the entrance hall camera. A large white shape moved from the front door through to the front room and there was himself, coming along from the kitchen to the front door, and so on.

"Oh! Oh my lord!" Gemma said as she watched. Her hands flicked from her mouth to her chest. "Is it...?"

"Actual, real, living footage of a ghost!" Oswin breathed. He longed to re-play it again, and watch it over and over, but his mother's voice called up the stairs, saying that it was time to go. He would have to wait for the whole weekend to pass before he could view his magnificent breakthrough again.

Chapter Seventeen

When Oswin's Dad dropped him back at the house the next evening, Beryl called him into the front room.

"Come and look!" she shrieked joyfully as he entered. Her eyes glistened and her cheeks were flushed. There in the centre of the window stood a huge Christmas tree. And all around it on the floor and on all the chairs were piles of ornaments and tinsel. All sorted out in groups of physical form and color. Beryl grinned and nodded at him, willing him to comment. It gave him an insight as to how Old Mother Hubbard felt when she came back home to find her little dog getting up to all sorts of tricks.

"Isn't it a bit early for that?" he asked in bewilderment, adjusting his spec's.

"Keep away from the baubles! Don't come any closer than that chair! The whole place is covered in breakable ornaments, mostly made of glass and other brittle materials. And I wouldn't want you to break any and hurt yourself," Beryl warned patronizingly.

Oswin thought that she rather *would* like it if he hurt himself.

"And no, it's not too early!" Beryl continued. "The shops have already started advertising Christmas long ago. And for me this run up to end of term is always hectic. For example, there's Gemma's dance concert that I always have to attend in place of our Mother God-Rest-Her-Soul, and my end of term tests, and now that I'm mixing with performing arts block students, I've got to work harder to prove myself. I can assure you, if you're not careful, before you know it, everyone else has got their trees up, and you're left looking like a fool."

"No one else in this street—or any other street that I'm familiar with—has put a tree up yet," he pointed out.

"Exactly! I'm not going to be the last one again this year. I'm going to be the first," Beryl replied, blushing at the memory of the previous Christmas shame. "And it's going to be the earliest, the biggest and the most beautifully decorated tree in the street."

Oswin frowned. "But won't it die before Christmas?"

"Excuse me!" Beryl rose up to her full height and placed her hands on her hips. "I beg your pardon! But as someone who has assumed the role of Mother Of The House for some years, I would think that by now I would know how to keep a Christmas tree alive for long enough! Now if you'll excuse me, I still have a lot of work to do. It takes a great deal of concentration to balance all the shapes and colors of the ornaments out. I've already spent two hours of my time getting this far and I've still got Geography homework to complete afterwards. So, thank you very much for all your concerned comments but I would prefer to be left alone to complete this enormous task with precision and care."

Oswin glared at her. "Oh, how we make you suffer!" he said quietly between his teeth and left the room.

He soon forgot Beryl's annoyance when he began watching the ghostly footage in his room. Although Gemma sadly informed him that there had been no strange activity during his absence, he was happy with that; he would have hated to miss anything now.

"It's an amazing breakthrough that we have this much!" he said with a grin. "Ghosts are very rarely caught on camera, you know." He ran his fingers through his hair and said, "But I see two of the cameras are down! Oh, well, never mind. I wasn't keen on those anyway."

They were the bedroom cameras and he decided to leave them off line and take them down completely as soon as he had a chance. He didn't need to peep and pry on others to get the footage he was looking for.

"Where are they placed, anyway?" Gemma asked.

"What? Oh, er...not in the kitchen, or the hall or front room," replied Oswin, blushing. He coughed and scratched his head before asking, "So...what night is your concert on, by the way?"

"Thursday," Gemma said. "And then on Friday night it's Rebecca's party."

"A party?"

"Yeah, you remember. The fancy dress party Rebecca Wilson's holding. I can go!" Gemma squeaked with joy and twirled around. "I'm going as Princess Fiona."

"That's really great!" smiled Oswin. "I'm glad your father finally let you go."

"Oh, he's not so strict as he makes out," Gemma assured him. "He even let Beryl talk him into putting up the Christmas tree early this year."

"Yes, I saw," was Oswin's tight-lipped reply.

"Bit early, huh?" Gemma said, wrinkling her nose in a good natured grimace. "I'm not over Halloween yet, myself. Not with the fancy dress party this week, but never mind! She promised not to switch the lights on until at least four weeks to Christmas."

* * * *

Even Beryl's boyfriend, Raj, was a little surprised when, on Thursday evening, he saw the great beauty dominating the front room. In an effort to show Beryl the family did indeed accept her boyfriend, Griswold encouraged her to bring Raj home. She brought him into the front room to show off a bit of *her* artistic abilities. Griswold was there, but was barely noticeable, because he had dozed off in his chair with the telly flickering and burbling soothingly in the background.

"Crikey Moses!" Raj exclaimed when he saw the Christmas tree. "What a brilliant tree!" He all but clapped his hands in glee.

Beryl ballooned with delight. It took her a full five seconds before she could overcome her emotions enough to reply, "Thank you, Raj. I appreciate your views on our Christmas tree. You know that Christmas is next month, don't you? I put it up and decorated it single-handed. That means all by myself. It took me six hours and fifteen minutes on Sunday."

"You don't say?" Raj was an amiable lad. Always ready with a complement. He said with genuine admiration, "But this shows great artistic talent!"

Beryl thought she would burst. She loved Raj very much.

And he had still more compliments to offer. "Have you ever thought of becoming a window dresser?"

"Not unless it takes a university degree," she replied. "Well, sit down, *darling*. Can I offer you some refreshments?"

"In here? What about those lyrics you wanted to show me?" he said, as Beryl pulled him down to sit beside her on the settee.

"Later, Raj, later. Let's just enjoy the tree for a little bit. Don't you think it's romantic, sitting here with the lights down and the tree sparkling?"

"Yes. Very," he replied then, thinking that didn't sound very convincing, he added, "And we must do it again when the tree is all lit up."

"Ooh, Raj!" breathed Beryl, snuggling up to him. Her lips sought his.

He sat up straight and stared at the tree. "Not in front of your old man! Please! I am very shy that way, you know!"

"But he's asleep! And besides he could only see us if he turned his head around deliberately to look at us. That's down to the way

I arranged the furniture," Beryl argued. "Don't be silly, Raj, just give us a little kiss!"

But her foghorn voice had roused Griswold from his sleep. He awoke with a snort.

"Huh? What's it?"

The love birds sprang apart. Raj broke out in a cold sweat, staring ahead, his back as stiff as an ironing board.

"It's alright, Father," said Beryl, in pronounced and loud tones. "You've been asleep, that's all. Raj and I—Beryl—are here with you, watching telly."

"Eh?" coughed Griswold gazing blearily around.

Beryl smiled knowingly at Raj, then spoke again to her father. "It's all right, Father, go back to sleep!"

But he shifted and rubbed his eyes and turned round to look at them. "What time is it? I have to pick Gemma up from the party. I mustn't over-sleep. I have to pick her up at ten."

"Raj and I are just going to the formal dining room—the one with the Van Gough—and we're going to study there, Father," said Beryl and she urged Raj to get up. Which he did, promptly.

"You haven't been sneaking the Christmas tree lights on, have you?" Griswold asked Beryl with narrowed eyes. "I'll find out if you have!"

Beryl gave a sharp cry of indignation. "No, of course not, Father! Have I put the lights on Raj? Even though you asked me to?"

Raj's eyes goggled. "No, not at all. Your Beryl has been very well behaved, Griswold!"

"Oh, alright then. Beryl make me a cuppa while you're up, there's a good girl?"

"Well, I have got homework to get on with, but I'll make you tea in a minute, Father!" she said and ushered Raj into the dining room.

* * * *

Griswold left early, at about half nine, to pick Gemma up from the fancy dress party. And no sooner had the front door clicked shut, than Beryl threw down her page of scribbled over lyrics and said, "We need a break from all this brainstorming!"

"Yeah, too right!" Raj said, almost knocking his chair over, he was so keen to stand up. He had not been able to get into the task at hand, had kept turning to look behind him. He was convinced on more than one occasion that he'd heard footsteps approaching. Plus, he found the room cold.

Chapter Eighteen

"Let's look at the Christmas tree again," Beryl said, leading Raj into the front room. "It's so beautiful, just to look at it cheers me up no matter how upset I am! And you know, all this work, work, work, can really get up my nose. It's so depressing! And creativity is supposed to be so easy! Ah, yes, this is better!"

She lit a joss stick and they sat staring at the tree for a few minutes, as the curling smoke fed the room with a rich and spicy scent, and Raj sighed.

"I can't wait to see the tree with the lights on."

"I know," said Beryl, her loud voice cracking through the peace, "but it's too early now. There's no way I can put them on yet. Sorry!"

"Yes, yes. Of course, I understand."

They sat in silence for a moment longer then Beryl jumped up.

"Oh, go on then, you've twisted my arm!" she blurted out. And before Raj could protest, she had switched the lights on. She had used three sets of lights, twisting them round the tree in a generous twinkling mass. And when the tree was aglow it was breathtaking. They both gasped and gazed.

"Don't feel bad about persuading me to put it on," said Beryl, shattering the silent awe. "I wanted to make sure they still worked properly. If one little light is out, you have to spend ages and ages trying to sort it out, finding that one culprit."

"You're really artistic," Raj murmured. "This tree is like—no *better* than—a picture on a Christmas card. It's breathtaking...so romantic!"

"Oh *Raj*!" Beryl sighed and before even she knew it they were in a clinch.

Naturally, they didn't notice the movement. A flash of shadow darted from the faux mantle place to the tree, whilst something scurried in a succession of jerks across the floor, as if under the carpet, in an agitated ripple. Both entities leapt up at the tree with the speed and force of an arrow shot from a bow. The tree swayed slightly. A burst of tremors ran through it as within its depths they scampered and scratched spitefully before finding the wires of the fairy lights. This only took a second and a half.

Beryl and Raj saw nothing of it, for it was one of those things best caught out of the corner of your eye—like a spider scuttling in the shadows—and Beryl and Raj were not looking. In fact, their eyes were closed as a spark zinged from the wires. Electricity, live and untamed, bolted through the delicate fabrics of the adorned tree and set it alight in less than a tick, the current was still clicking as the first flames were born. Flames which bred with lightning speed, crackling through the tree and the sparks, unhindered. The shadowy entities which had caused all the mischief fled—obscure movements darting amongst the shadows of the evening.

Still,Beryl and Raj, eyes shut and arms entwined, were blissfully locked away from the crisis unravelling around them. Indeed, Raj mistook the gooseflesh running up his spine, the crackling sensation around him, for the first pangs of true love.

It was Oswin who, up in his room, was alerted by the momentary dimming of the lights. His eyes focused immediately on his monitor. He could see a white flash darting from the tree, but this sighting was upstaged by the horror of the flames licking greedily at the delicate foliage. He didn't even notice Raj and Beryl snogging on the couch.

Grabbing his Ghost-O-Meter he raced downstairs, pausing in the hallway only long enough to wrench a bouquet of flowers from its vase and carried the vessel of water through to the front room.

Upon entering it, he pulled the trigger of his Ghost-O-Meter and tossed the contents of vase clumsily at the tree. There was less water than needed to douse the flames devouring the tree, but more than enough to kill the fire of passion raging within the couple on the settee, for the water landed more on Beryl and Raj than on the tree and the splash was coupled with the *"Wheeeeeeee... click...click...click...pop!"* of the meter. Beryl was too shocked to protest for a moment.

As Raj and Beryl blinked the water from their eyes, coughing and spluttering as their senses returned to dull reality, they were awakened to the crisis at hand. With Oswin's help, they sort of managed to put the burning tree out. Raj kept crying out, "Smother it, don't douse it! Water's bad on electric fires!"

Beryl danced about, her arms in the air as she yelled, "My tree! My tree!" She looked like a priestess ceremoniously evoking a god.

The fire alarm went off, drowning their cries and adding to the sense of confusion as they scrambled for a something with which to smother the flames. With every second they took, the fire increased in size and ferocity. They had to use the settee cushions to smother it and this ruined both the tree and the lounge suite.

They just about got the fire put out when the fire brigade arrived, and in its wake came Griswold and Gemma, who was still green from the party. They all had to go and stand on the front lawn, while the fire brigade were busy in the house. Neighbors came out and stood on their doorsteps, staring openly at the family. Beryl and Raj, particularly, shivered in the night air. The party glared at one another in the darkness, standing still in their varying degrees of shock and bewilderment, as the fire brigade moved efficiently around them. One or two of the heroic men paused long enough to cast astonished looks at Gemma. She didn't seem to notice, although Griswold coughed and stared at his feet each time.

"Did you set the tree on fire, Oswin?" Beryl asked after some time. She had procured a blanket, which she'd wrapped around her like an oversized dressing gown.

"No!" Oswin snapped.

"Only it seemed perfectly all right to me. One moment it was fine, the next moment, you were shooting it with your ray gun and throwing water over Raj and I. I have my suspicions about all this, you know! Those lights were not faulty. There was no way they would have burst into flames on their own."

"But..."

"Beryl!" Griswold said, "That's a terrible thing to say. The boy..."

"Hear me out now, Father! I'm not saying he *tried* to burn the house down." At these words she turned patronizingly to Oswin. "You know that's not what I was saying. I know you wouldn't do a thing as naughty as that. However, what I think is that it's a practical joke gone wrong. I think you got the toy ray gun to actually work. And you shot at my Christmas tree."

"That's ridiculous!" Griswold said. "There's no such thing as a ray gun!"

Bristling, Beryl stood her ground. "Let me have my say! I've had a traumatic evening, having to watch my tree and all that hard work of six and a quarter hours of decorating it, go up in flames and I'm having trouble coping with it all..."

"I'd say," Oswin muttered.

Gemma caught his eye and giggled.

"Stop interrupting me," Beryl demanded angrily. "I'm going to finish what I've got to say, whether you like it or not! I mean, Father, that Oswin is a gifted child there's no doubt. You do know you're especially clever, don't you Oswin?"

Oswin glared at her.

"Well, you know how fond of the gun he is, Father!" Beryl said, before turning upon Oswin again. "You can't deny it, Oswin, we've all been shot by you with your toy ray gun. I of course, have born the brunt of your ray gun assaults, although I can't think why. But what I'm saying is that I believe you have the capability to build something such as a real working ray gun..."

At this Raj and Oswin and Gemma broke into a fit of giggles.

Griswold rolled his eyes and gave a grunt of mirthless laughter. "There is no such thing as a ray gun, Beryl. That's Seventies science fiction gobbledygook! You'll probably find the fire's all down to faulty wiring."

"There was nothing the matter with my Christmas tree lights! Oswin came in and set fire to the tree with a homemade plasma energy torpedo burst from the gun he carries about with him all the time."

"Plasma energy?" Griswold asked, looking a tad doubtful.

"Yes! This fire's caused by plasma energy bursts!" Beryl declared loudly. "You should be saying how grateful you are that he didn't aim his weapon at me, Father, like he usually does! It would be me—the Mother Figure of this household—that had burst into flames. And how would you like that, Father? Eh? With no one to cook and clean for you and to take care of little Gemma?"

Griswold tugged at his moustache. "You've not been experimenting with plasma energy, have you, boy?" he asked.

"No!" said Oswin. "That's *Nineties* science fiction gobbledygook."

Their noisy debate was cut short by the approach of the fire chief and he told them it was down to faulty Christmas lights.

"Never had a Christmas tree fire this early in the year," he remarked. "And all your cameras and some of your wall sockets have shorted out. Better get someone in to look at the house's wiring."

"Nonsense!" Beryl argued. "I'm sorry, but that's a lazy explanation! You see a burnt up Christmas tree and you conclude, without an investigation, that it's faulty fairy lights—how unimaginative! Well, I'll have you know, Inspector Fire Chief, that those lights were not on at the time that the fire occurred."

"I think you'll find they were, Miss," the man replied, undaunted. "Most of these fires occur through lights being put on and forgotten—left unattended."

"No! This one wasn't. I have a witness. Raj and I were both in the front room at the time of the fire and I think *you'll* find that he'll back me up when I say the lights were very definitely off."

"But Baby mine," Raj blurted innocently, "you must be in shock. Don't you remember? You'd put them on to show me how beautiful..."

"You put the lights on already?" Griswold gasped. "You were allowed to put the tree up on the sole condition that you wait..."

"Raj! How *could* you? That is extreme unfaithfulness, that is! If those lights were on—and I'm not saying they were, because I don't remember them being on—but *if* they were on, it was because Raj insisted on seeing them. In fact, he *made* me put them on. That's twice in one evening, Raj, that you have not had my best interests at heart." Beryl sniffed luxuriously, wiping her nose on the blanket, and implored shakily. "Oh, I'm so hurt! No one believes me, and I *know* what happened!"

Raj gasped. "I think she's lost it a bit! Honestly Griswol...Mister MacPherson, I think it's the shock of it all. She doesn't mean it." He asked the fireman if they could go back into the house. "Beryl needs to lie down, and have some strong tea," he said. "She's lost her mind, she's not well."

"She's done enough lying already," Griswold muttered, red in the face.

"Yes, you can go back in," the fireman assured them. "You seem to have most of your electricity working but some of your downstairs sockets have gone. And all those cameras—even the ones upstairs—are all shot. Some of their wires have melted. You're lucky the whole place didn't go up in a show of sparks. I strongly advise you to get the wiring thoroughly checked. You know how these old houses can be!"

Raj was keen to carry the ailing Beryl up to bed, but she wouldn't let him touch her.

"No! I'm sorry," she insisted forcibly, tears brimming angrily. "I can't have you touch me! After such a betrayal, such blatant disloyalty, I couldn't have you come near me again. I could never trust you!"

She huffed up to her bedroom unattended and slammed the door.

"Let me go after her," Raj said. "Let me explain."

"Little point in that...er...Raj. She'll not hear you. Not in that state," Griswold said. He surveyed the he front room. "*Crikey,* look at this mess!"

"The tree!" Raj groaned. "Beryl will be crushed when she sees it! It'll wipe her out!"

"Heavens, boy, you're right!" Griswold breathed. There was a hollow look in his face. "We'd better get it out of here, quick!"

"But not the whole thing, surely? I think some ornaments can be saved!"

Griswold shook his head. "The whole bloody lot, boy...er...Raj." Then he rubbed his hands and adopted a brisker pose. "Oswin, you get the dustpan! And a damp cloth. Raj, you and I get this lot packed in the trailer, ready for the dump. The settee may as well go too. Gemma..." He gazed dismally at Gemma. "You look like a bleeding Muppet—get that green paint off your face and go straight to bed! You've got school in the morning."

Oswin sneaked a couple of readings with his 'ray gun' while sweeping and mopping up, although he had missed the crucial period.

"Still," he muttered to himself, "it's obviously falling from a peak."

Griswold and Raj caught him with the meter in his hands.

"Oswin! For Pity's Sake! Put that gun away, it's caused enough trouble for one night!" Griswold barked. "As soon as you're finished it's off to bed with you too! It's getting late. Cor, what a night!" He rubbed a weary hand over his face.

Raj asked, "Please, Mister MacPherson, can I try to speak to Beryl?"

"Eh? Oh, all right, then, if she'll let you."

Raj ran up the stairs and begged Beryl to listen to him, but his efforts were to no avail. He tapped on Beryl's door for ten minutes, calling her in his soft voice while Griswold watched from the landing.

"You betrayed me, you *Judas*, I'm too upset to discuss this any further," Beryl sobbed from her bed at last.

Raj frowned. "No, it's me, *Raj!* Open the door, I want to talk to you!"

But she wouldn't; she complained in loud wail, "I've been stabbed in the back by Brutus! That's what!"

"I am not a brute," Raj protested. "Oh, please let me talk to you! Let me comfort you!"

But he could not get her to open the door.

Eventually Griswold intervened. "I think you'd better go, son. There's nothing you can do now," he said. And so Raj went, with his head down and his shoulders drooping.

Oswin, in contrast, was positively perky. Griswold was

annoyed to see Gemma loitering in the boy's room in her Pyjamas and gown, brushing her long, loose hair.

"Gemma! What are you doing? That's enticing to men, that is!"

"What?" blinked Gemma. Her eyes were red and she still had a green smudge by her left ear.

"Eh?" Oswin muttered, barely looking from his monitor. "Look at this, Uncle! I've caught the exact moment the fire started on screen."

"Did you indeed, son? Well, now let's see this," Griswold replied, rubbing his hands together.

Chapter Nineteen

An hour or so later, after intense discussion and amazing revelations, Griswold was congratulating himself on being able to finally get to bed, when, as he passed Beryl's door, he heard her still crying.

"Aw, come on, Beryl," he said, peeping in. "You're not still upset are you?"

She lifted her head heavily and gazed vaguely towards him. Her eyes were barely visible in her face—red and swollen with crying. Her hair was dishevelled and her clothes crumpled. And as she moaned and began to rock herself, she looked like a hideous, misshapen beast.

"Good gracious, girl! What's happened to you!" Griswold cried and this set her off in a fresh bout of sobs. He fussed over her as she lay on her bed moaning and crying inconsolably, until, in the early hours of the morning, he rang up and persuaded their family doctor to come out and look at her.

The doctor was very abrupt and injected her as roughly as he could with a tranquilliser. Beryl was horrified, as she thought she should have been admitted into hospital with a nervous break down, and told him so angrily.

"I shall file a complaint! Why haven't you rushed me to casualty, yet? My head is about to burst, it's so swollen—I can feel it—it's the size of a melon! No one appreciates that I am under *enormous* stress here, with added burdens..." And—*pop!*—she fell asleep. The doctor muttered irritably under his breath as he stomped back home to bed.

* * * *

The next morning, the others put off facing Beryl with unspoken bliss. It was peaceful to the point of euphoria after the scenes of the previous night, as they set about the final tasks of clearing up. Griswold took time off work to catch up on his sleep and to make trips to the dump. Gemma and Oswin flipped through the Yellow Pages over a bowl of cornflakes, looking for an electrician, before seeing themselves, unhindered, off to school while Beryl slept like a monstrous baby. Bliss!

She had to awake at some point. As soon as she regained her strength, she called a family meeting in the front room. Her black nail varnish and skull ring were gone. Instead she wore her hair pinned up into a tight, efficient bun and was sporting a pair of horn rimmed glasses. Oswin had serious doubts as to whether their lenses were more than plain glass. Beryl stood beside one of the new settee's arms and held a clipboard and a pen.

"We need to talk about banning homemade battery operated toys," Beryl said. "As has been demonstrated to us, they can be lethal." She gave Oswin a pointed stare. "We could have burnt to our deaths. Not to mention the tree. I put six and a quarter hours of effort into decorating it. I loved that tree like a child. Yes, that's actually how it was for me. And now it's... Well, I'm over the worst of my loss, but I can assure you, I will always bear the scars."

"We're sorry the tree burnt down," Gemma said. "But Oswin has something terrific to show you."

"Excuse me! I beg your pardon! But I don't want to see Oswin's latest inventions. I don't know if you can understand that, Gemma, but it is a sore point for me at the moment. I lost my Christmas tree and my boyfriend, who happened to be the best one I've ever had. Until, that is, that moment of betrayal, which split my chest open and ripped my heart out..."

"All right, all right," Griswold snapped, his moustache bristling irritably, "Beryl, listen to this..."

"Excuse me! I beg your pardon, Father, but I'm not going to allow anyone to override my feelings on this matter. I want you all to know how I feel about this situation. It's important to me that you do."

"But the point is the fire..."

"Exactly! That fire has caused me two great losses. One: the pain of losing all that I had put into decorating the tree, and the ornaments, so lovingly collected and kept. Some of those are from the time when Mother, May-She-Rest-in-Peace, was still with us, you know, so that's an added loss. That's all gone, wiped out by the fire. And two: the loss of my boyfriend. I've not only had to cope with the relationship there coming to an abrupt and painful end, but also with an immense betrayal. He wouldn't have betrayed me if it weren't for the fire. And how was the fire caused?"

"Exactly!" Gemma squeaked, dancing quick little steps on her toes, until Griswold pulled her by the arm to a chair and made her sit down.

"That's what we're trying to tell you. It wasn't Oswin's gun," he said. "That isn't even a gun. It..."

"I beg your pardon! Are you saying that the fairy lights were to blame? They were not! I didn't spend six and a quarter hours on that tree just to put in faulty fairy lights. They were of the best quality. I checked each bulb individually. Yes, I am that thorough...*Let me finish!*...and they were all working fine and the wire had no nicks."

"I am glad that you are so sure," Oswin said, his steady words managing to halt Beryl's rapid flow. "I hope that you will be willing to sign a testimony to that effect. Because we don't think it was the lights either."

"Then it was..."

"No. It wasn't my Ghost-O-Meter. Watch this!"

Oswin set the film recording on play before Beryl could volley another assault of words at them. The screen on the telly showed a wordless scene of Beryl and Raj snuggling up on the telly, of Beryl switching on the Christmas tree lights, and the inevitable clinch. Beryl's face paled then flushed a deeper and deeper red. Her mouth gaped open and shut a few times before she managed to find her tongue.

"Oh, hold on a minute! What's this? A camera? You've been filming me?" she demanded. "Did you know it's illegal to spy on people like that. I'm going to our lawyer. I'm going to sue you if you've been secretly filming me."

"Wait!" they all cried. "Look!"

Oswin froze the picture. "See this little white field of energy?" he said, using a pencil to point it out on the screen. "Watch it, now. Plus another one will appear from here. Now watch!...See? They're both on the tree and..." The first sparks sprayed across the screen and the fire took hold.

"What are those little white smudges?" Beryl asked.

"Ghosts," Griswold replied, "poltergeists."

"Or fairies," Gemma whispered. "Gremlins."

"They are the energy fields of two entities. They didn't show up on the camera themselves, but their energy fields did," Oswin explained. "See you and Raj? That light haze around you are your energies—sort of like a magnetic field. It's weaker than these. My theory is that ghosts are all energy field and no body, whereas we are all body and not much energy field."

"Body and soul!" Gemma gasped. "Body and spirit. Our soul,

our spirit is contained inside us. We are flesh but they are spirit only."

Beryl folded her arms. "I don't know if I can believe this," she declared.

"Show her the salt cellar incident," Griswold said.

Oswin ran the scene in the kitchen-diner and they all watched as the little white smudge zoomed down from the clock, scurried across the table and hurled itself at the salt cellar, toppling it over, then leapt straight back up to the clock.

"See? I told you so!" Beryl cried. "My hands were nowhere near the cellar!" She looked triumphantly at the others. "Yeah! This spy camera works both ways, you know. Now I've been cleared on that account outright. Father, you have to admit my hands did not even come close to touching..."

Griswold sighed. "Yes, all right, Beryl, you didn't knock it over!"

"Here's another one. This is a different sort of ghost. A spectral ghost. She came in soon after the salt cellar. Remember we all thought we heard my Mum coming? Well, it wasn't... See that hazy figure? Look, a few moments later...and there she is. See the differences in energy fields? She's bigger and you can trace the outline of a human figure. Watch as she goes into the front room. Here I come...I'll speed this up to normal pace for you...I just miss her. And as you know, when we went into the room there was nothing there. The field detecting camera there didn't even switch on."

"But no one was accused of anything then," Beryl said.

"It's not about blaming anyone for anything. He caught a ghost on camera, Beryl," Gemma said. "That's very hard to do."

"It's them little buggers that shorted the wiring and started the fire," Griswold said.

"Yes," agreed Oswin. "And I'll bet they did it deliberately. They never liked the cameras."

"Hang on a minute," Beryl said, her eyes narrowed. "How long did you have the cameras up? Father, were you aware that we were all being filmed? Why haven't you said anything about it?" she demanded.

"Well...I...er..."Griswold squirmed. "It was sort of my idea. But look what we have; actual footage of real ghosts. I bet you that's worth a fortune, eh?"

"Stick to the point, Father," Beryl reminded him firmly. "You were having us filmed in our rooms, in our private moments."

"I kept that down to a bare minimum," Oswin pointed out,

nudging his glasses up. "I was far more interested in capturing the ghosts..."

"I was well and truly worried with all that joss stick burning," Griswold interrupted in his defence.

Gemma sighed. "I don't mind!"

"There!" said Griswold. "Gemma doesn't mind. She's got nothing to hide."

"And neither do I," Beryl cried. "But I resent this invasion into my privacy!"

"I was worried that you were smoking pot," her father insisted. "I thought...er...Raj may be influencing you..."

"Huh! That betraying little Emo wouldn't smoke anything, yet alone illegal substances. Grade C or not! All that heavy metal, gothic rock is just a show with him and his silly little band!"

"Yes," Griswold ducked his head. "I know that now. I should never have doubted you..."

"Exactly! I am totally innocent. I never did drugs and I never started the fire. My lights were not faulty!" Beryl said triumphantly. "Now, as to the illegal surveillance. You have disabled the cameras, haven't you? Good! Meeting adjourned!"

"But what about the ghosts?" Gemma said.

"What? The ghosts? Yes, of course the little white things started the fire, and ruined my precious tree. Did I tell you I spent six and-a-quarter hours putting it up? Plus, they had me falsely accused of knocking over the salt cellar *and* they ultimately ruined my relationship with Raj. And who knows what else." She paused and narrowed her eyes. "I have a vague memory of my Coast sweater being found in the toilet, or was that all a nightmare? Nevertheless, we must call someone to exterminate the little horrors. Father, I don't know how you can allow us live in a ghost-infested house. No wonder poor Gemma is not in touch with reality!"

Beryl phoned a directory service straight away and told the story in the longest possible way to each person she spoke to on her route to finding a ghost buster.

First she explained her cause in unnecessary detail to the directory assistant, then to the secretary of National Society for Psychical Research, and finally to a certain Mister Philip Westworth, the man who would lead any investigation into Oswin's inventions and discovery. Each time her story became more her own and more graphic.

"I don't want you to laugh at me, Mister Westworth," she said.

"We've actually got proof of this, in the form of CCTV footage—genuine stuff. I've been feeling very uneasy lately. I put it all down to the stress of running a home, fostering my little cousin who we look after during the week, and being a mother figure to Gemma, my little sister—our mother has passed on, you see—all this on top of keeping up with my school work! It seems I have also been the victim of reign of terror imposed upon me by a poltergeist. Yes! A pair of poltergeists, no less! No wonder my head feels like it wants to explode!"

Oswin bristled in the background. He tried to wrestle the receiver out of Beryl's hand, but she kept him at arm's length by placing a firm hand on his forehead. After flailing about for some time, Oswin had to content himself with pacing back and forth, trying to launch surprise attacks on Beryl. All of which were more than unsuccessful, Beryl was hardly put out of her stride.

"No! Whatever makes you think this is a prank call?" she protested into the receiver. "Excuse me! *Excuse me!* I'll have you know that a serious study of the situation has already been conducted in..."

Oswin groaned. "Do something!" he pleaded to Griswold.

"...my cousin, who is a gifted child... Alright, then. The point is that we want you to come and have a look at the house, to at least confirm our findings. I am sure you will see what I am talking about the minute you walk into the house, and then of course, if you could remove the ghosts...oh!...Well, yes, I know Ghost Busters wasn't real, but..." There was a long pause, before Beryl spoke again. "I am well aware of that!...well, if you could simply make an appointment to...I'll hand you over to Father. He's a company manager, you know—in charge of a lot of people."

Griswold, coming up behind Beryl, wrenched the phone from her and took over the conversation.

Chapter Twenty

After speaking with Griswold, it was arranged that Mister Westworth would come on Saturday. The entire household had given up work, study, dancing, and family togetherness to be there. Mister Westworth brought with him a psychic medium called Patricia and a technically-minded gentleman called Gary, who had gadgets of his own. He was very interested in the Ghost-O-Meter, although he could not have failed to notice that it looked and sounded like a toy space gun.

"Wow, this is a brilliant little invention!" he enthused. "Have you thought of having it patented? I suggest you do. I know it's a long and laborious process—it may even take years, but it's well worth it, son!"

Although Patricia didn't want to be told a thing of the haunting prior to her investigation, Mister Westworth and Gary spent a long time going through the ghost diary. Then both men sat in Oswin's room and studied the ghostly footage and all his notes on how he adapted the camera. They even took Gemma's ghost diary seriously.

Meanwhile, Patricia wandered through the house with a quartz crystal wand, making her own notes and standing for long periods in various rooms and crannies. She had very long hair, a husky voice and huge blue eyes. Griswold took an instant liking to her and trailed after her on her rounds. Beryl distrusted Patricia instantly and also followed her.

"To make sure," she hissed noisily into Gemma's ear, "nothing goes missing!"

Gemma blushed scarlet, convinced that the medium heard, but if she did, Patricia ignored Beryl grandly and placed a cool hand on Gemma's arm.

"Come with me," she said and she flittered from room to room with her entourage of hosts hovering near. She stopped in the front room, breathed in deeply a few times and circled the room. The party drew back slightly, wide-eyed and silent, as she lifted her head and let her eyes roll back before they fluttered closed.

"It is difficult to pinpoint any one thing," Patricia breathed. "This room has been a focal point for dwellers of the house since its origin." Here Beryl rolled her eyes and Patricia, apparently having not seen her, continued. "Being the front room, of course that is to be expected. It holds layers of strong emotions...layers!"

"That's funny," Griswold mused. "Our Gemma never spends too much time in here. She just comes to watch a bit of telly. But it's the dining room she *really...*"

Patricia's eyes flew open and met his. He blushed and turned away.

"There is a sense of loneliness, of waiting, that is particularly strong for me," she went on. "Perhaps someone spent many hours grieving for a loved one here, or waiting...hoping for their return."

"If you get a sense of a lot of bereavement up in my room," said Beryl, "that would be me the other night. I had no choice but to break up with my boyfriend. I was betrayed, you know."

"It has a sense of great loneliness," said Patricia, continuing to ignore Beryl. "Sometimes souls get lost in a period of their lives. It is such an intense time for them that even after death they are drawn back to it. Sometimes a person can pull a departed loved one back, creating an earth-bound spirit. Other times a person can hold *themselves* down on earth."

"You're not saying one of us is keeping my late wife here?" gasped Griswold. "I was...very fond of her! I still miss her, but I'm used to her being gone."

Patricia smiled at him and placed a hand on his burning cheek. "Your darling Minnie sends her love and misses you too. But no, she is not haunting this house, she is at great peace. She also says thank you for the rose bush you planted in her name and also, you should try to be less uptight and she hopes you find love again."

Griswold gulped and suddenly found his shoes very interesting.

"I think we could have been soul mates," Beryl said, sniffing.

Patricia made notes, jotting them down in a decorated note book, and they passed on to the hall. This, she explained was similar to the front room and for the same reasons. It was beginning to seem like a tour of a house from a quirky estate agent. When they walked into the dining room, Patricia gasped. She paled and whimpered, becoming clearly distracted for a moment.

"Are you alright, luv?" asked Griswold, placing a hand on the medium's shoulder.

Patricia's eyes did that rolling thing again and her voice was jagged and even huskier than ever. "There is..someone...something here. Is it fury, or the presence of evil?"

"You're not going to go into a trance on us, are you?" Beryl asked anxiously. "I don't think I could handle stuff like that..." She broke off and giggled nervously, glancing from Patricia to Griswold and to Gemma. But no one responded to her. She sighed heavily and hung back moodily.

"We hardly ever use this room," Gemma said at last. "It's too cold, and formal, and...uncomfortable...to eat in."

Patricia did not respond immediately. She put her hands out, "There is an emptiness..." she breathed, "something stolen...missing..." She stopped dead in her tracks and her eyes opened very wide. "There," she pointed to the wall, where the framed print hung. The glass was cracked in two places.

"That's just a print of a Van Gough," said Beryl. "I got it at a charity shop. It keeps falling down. I've hung it up twice last month..."

"It's gone from there," Patricia interrupted in a frightened shriek. "...such anger...hatred!" She swayed slightly and Griswold, moving for the first time since entering the room, rushed to support her.

"Whatever are you going on about?" Beryl asked. "Excuse me! But I think you're frightening Gemma."

"The clock," Gemma breathed. "You moved the clock from there."

"No, hang on a minute," Beryl said. "I don't like where this is going! It's not as though I stole it. As Mother-of-the-House I made a decision to move it. It's only in the kitchen. I just put it there because that's where we all eat. It's a kitchen-*diner*! It's nice to have a clock there. And Father wouldn't buy a new one, so I moved this one."

"Would you like a cup of tea...er...Pat?" Griswold asked tenderly, steering Patricia out towards the kitchen.

"I had no *choice* but to move it!" Beryl stamped her foot and sniffed as everyone else hurried to the kitchen. It seemed they were glad for an excuse to leave the dining room.

Beryl hurried up from the rear of the party, crying, "Wait for me! Here, let *me* put the kettle on!"

She quickly found her feet again, in ordering Gemma and Griswold about with regards to looking after the trembling Patricia. "Put her down at the table, Father. Gemma, get some biscuits. Nothing with icing, nothing too rich—digestives!"

Patricia allowed herself to be placed in one of the kitchen table chairs, and, still shivering, clasped a mug of sweet tea gratefully. Just as it seemed that she was regaining her balance, she gasped, and let out a rasping scream. Everyone followed her gaze. It was on the clock.

"It's in there," she breathed, pointing to the clock, her tea sloshing onto the table. The others froze, unsure of what to do.

"Oh, my gawd!" Beryl hooted. "She's not going all funny again, is she? She's going to throw a fit! Gemma, boil some more water!"

Gemma obeyed, although she couldn't think what Beryl was going to do with more hot water. Still, it gave her something to do—something better to focus on than on poor Patricia, who continued to stare unseeingly at the clock, gaping, like a fish out of water.

Griswold gently patted her back and said, "There, there!" He began to rub her back in gentle little circles—soothingly—despite Beryl glaring primly at him.

There was a long silence, magnifying the hiss of the kettle.

At last Patricia the medium swallowed and spoke. "Attached to that clock is a presence—No! I sense two, two presences—and they want to be in the dining room."

"That's not *our* family clock, or anything," Griswold hastened to explain, and stopped rubbing her back. "It came with the house. I was so surprised the previous owners left it, I even phoned them to make sure they hadn't forgotten it."

"Do you think they left it because they were frightened of it?" asked Gemma.

"I wouldn't be surprised," Patricia said faintly. "And I know that you would have fewer strange disturbances once you move that clock back to the dining room!"

"Perhaps we should get rid of it altogether," said Griswold, crossing purposefully towards the clock.

"Now hang on a minute!" Beryl shrieked, dashing to bar his way. "I don't like you talking that way about my clock! That's a valuable family heirloom. We've got precious little of that sort of thing. I don't think we should be getting rid of our assets. It is our family clock now and I'm proud to own it."

"It contains a presence, that has been disturbed and is angry," Patricia repeated quietly. She put her fingers to her temples and shut her eyes.

"Oh, she's off again," Beryl muttered irritably, but Griswold shot her such a stern look, she almost blushed.

Patricia said in her dusky, husky tones, "My guide is telling me that there are two dryads attached to the clock—they are the spirits of the tree from which it was carved. When the tree was felled, instead of moving on, the hamadryads stayed with the fallen tree...they continue to live in the wood...they're still furious at having been cut down..." Her voice trailed off but her lips moved rapidly. Griswold, Beryl and Gemma looked at each other, at Patricia, then back at each other.

After a pause, Patricia opened her eyes with a gasp and instantly resumed her usual composure, smiling at Griswold and the girls. "I urged them to move over to the other side too, to follow the light and find peace, but..."

"They get to go to Heaven?" Griswold asked incredulously.

Patricia blinked. "Well, yes. All living things have a spirit and ultimately belong with God in Heaven."

"With my wife? You sent them up there with my dear departed wife?"

Patricia shook her head patiently. "Don't worry, Griswold, no harm will ever come to your wife in Heaven. Besides," she continued with a sigh, "to be honest with you, I'm not sure that the dryads have left this plane yet."

"Oh, so they're being picky now, are they? Cheeky beggars!"

"Yes," Beryl added, "if they want to stay in my clock in my house, they'll have to put up with whatever room I choose..."

At this the dining room door slammed with such velocity that the whole house shook. The Van Gough crashed to the floor with a tinkling of shattering glass and the clock slid, scraping, from the wall and thudded onto the kitchen table with a *Twaangg-Wanggg!* of shaken springs. Then, over the hush that followed, its clockwork continued unabated, louder than usual...tick...tock... tick...and with an air of menace. Even though the pendulum was not moving!

As one, the party stepped back away from the table, gooseflesh rippling across their backs, up their necks and sending icy tendrils over their scalps. The color drained from even Beryl's face and she was noticeably silent.

Steps thudded down the staircase and Oswin, Gary and Mister Westworth sprang into the kitchen—all their gismos aimed and loaded.

"*Wheeeeeeee...click...click....click...pop!*" and a quieter, "*Grrrrrr...tukatukatukatuk...*" resounded through the room and was followed by another moment of astonished silence.

"Oh, all right!" Beryl snapped. "I'll just move it back to it's old space, then! There's no need to get all hysterical about it! It was only a suggestion that it live here. I had to make that decision to move it. Besides, no one protested at the time."

She pushed through the scientists, huddled in a frenzy of examination, and yanked the clock unceremoniously from the table, stomping off to the dining room with it.

"That girl!" Griswold muttered, rubbing his forehead distractedly as they listened to angry crunching of shoes on glass.

"Look at this!" Gary muttered and Westworth and Oswin nodded, conferred with him, discussing temperature fluctuations and the static.

Gemma shrugged and smiled awkwardly at Patricia.

"Come, Gemma," Patricia said. "Why don't you come around with me while I do a bit of spiritual cleansing for your house. I don't mind *you* helping me. Then perhaps, afterwards, we can all have a cup of tea."

When they were out of earshot of the others she said, "Gemma, I've been able to pick up some information from the housewife ghost you told me about. She's not just your imagination, but she's not threatening, like the hamadryads. Her name was Vera and she lived here all her married life. I know because I have made contact with her through my spirit guide, and urged her to go over. It's very sad, her son went missing in action during the war. She always hoped he'd return, knitting jumper after jumper for him, listening for the knock on the door."

"I've often seen her!"

Patricia nodded. "Even long after D Day, she could never accept that he would not come home. She was always waiting for him. You were able to see her because you have a gift. Like me, you're psychic—able to see spirits. Yes, you are, although you'd no idea, I assume, of the existence and power of Spirit. If you are interested, it's a talent which you can develop. But that's up to you. As for Vera, she says she is sorry to have frightened you, Gemma."

Gemma ducked her head briefly. "So, her name's Vera? I didn't mean to be such a baby. I suppose I should have felt that she wasn't unfriendly."

"But you did, really, didn't you? I think as you become used to your gift, you'll be more comfortable with it." Patricia smiled as Gemma helped her pack away her crystal and cleansing water. Gemma especially liked the crystal. It was cool and strong and deep.

"Will I get a guide, like you?" she asked, holding the crystal in the palms of her hands and letting the smooth surface cool her skin.

"Yes, I'm sure of it, but only if you let him or her in. Spirit will never force itself on you. Like I said, it's up to you, if you want to explore your psychic abilities."

"Did Vera say why she was here, haunting this house?" Gemma asked, at last handing the stone back.

"It's just that she was happy here. She loved her home so dearly that she wants to stay on," explained Patricia, zipping her bag shut. Then she leaned forward and tweaked Gemma's chin. "She also thinks she should stick around to keep you safe from those hamadryads. She says she knows them from when she was alive here and they can be nasty. She says she won't cross over until they've gone."

Chapter Twenty One

Meanwhile, Mister Westworth and Gary spoke with Oswin as they wound down their investigation. Although they took an interest in his inventions, it was not all good news.

"It's splendid that we got a chance to see your Ghost-O-Meter in action, and you saw how ours works," said Gary. "Ours is more bulky, as it prints out the recordings. And," he added with a twinkle in his eye, "it's not so imaginative."

Oswin grinned. "The Ghost-O-Meter used to look more like a remote control. But it burnt out. When I built it up, stronger, I also disguised it as a toy gun, so that Beryl and Griswold would leave it alone."

Westworth smiled dryly. "Yes, I can understand that."

"You have a good theory," Gary remarked, "and it should be developed. Many scientists, myself included, are thinking down those lines."

"About the equipment," asked Mister Westworth, "did you make it unaided?"

"Yeah, but I need a bit of help with the cameras," Oswin replied, pulling out his notes. "They all shorted out. What could I do to prevent that happening so easily?"

Mister Westworth glanced at them, but explained that he didn't think it was worth the effort to bother too much with cameras at this stage. "You see," he said, handing them back to Oswin, "the thing is that camera footage wouldn't be taken seriously, even if you did get them up and running again."

"Little white misty blobs on camera look highly suspicious to the sceptical eye," Gary explained, placing his lap top in its case. "Especially as there are countless hoax films and photos of so called ghosts. I can run thorough tests to prove to myself and some others that they are genuine recordings of ghostly activity, Oswin, but you might just as well be Christopher Columbus trying to prove his 'Earth is round' theory. Sure, the media would love this sort of thing, but for all the wrong reasons."

"And your being so young won't help people take you seriously," Mister Westworth added, picking his brief case up. He suggested that Oswin keep on amassing evidence, and experimenting with detecting devices. "But until you have a qualification, a degree, in science—as I am sure you will in the future—you are unlikely to convince anyone but a few like-minded ghost hunters," he finished.

"Like Columbus," Gary added. "One day the world will be convinced and you'll be believed. But that day is yet to come. Until then, the more serious you are about the existence of ghosts, and that sort of dimension, the less seriously you'll be taken. You'll be a nutter in the eyes of the public and the world of science. They'll continually try to catch you out and expose you as a fool or a fraud."

"But I'm not!" Oswin cried. "This is all genuine equipment, and disciplined recordings."

"Yes," Mister Westworth said. "But they'll be implying that you've let yourself be duped, that you're an eccentric anorak case. It's tough out there, Oswin, we've been through it ourselves. And look at the household you live in. Imagine that bunch on camera. It'll be a pantomime!"

"Gemma's alright," Oswin said folding his arms. "So she's a little quirky, but that's all part of her charm."

"I know, but the media and science are harsh critics. Gemma is definitely clairvoyant, but sadly, that's a minus point as far as the media goes. And as she's a little quirky in her manner, they'll make fun of her."

"If you go public with this equipment and evidence now, the media will rip your story to shreds," Mister Westworth put in.

"Ghosts do exist!" Oswin declared. He ran his fingers through his hair and clenched the straight strands so tightly it pulled.

"Yes," Gary agreed, "and the world is round. But you'll have to wait for everybody else to catch up with you, yeah?"

Oswin frowned for a moment then folded his arms, unfolded them and adjusted his specs. "Yeah," he sighed with a shrug. "I suppose you're right."

"You've got years ahead of you to study and develop your theories," Mister Westworth said, placing a hand on his shoulder, "and your detecting gadgets. Keep ghost hunting, Oswin. Develop new ways of detecting and analyzing ghosts. It may become a new science in your lifetime but it's not recognized yet." His car keys jangled in his hand as he waved goodbye to Oswin.

And that, as Oswin said later, was about it. Gemma still saw Vera, the ghost, but she was no longer frightened by her. In fact, she began to find it comforting to see Vera knitting away at that dull brown yarn, or plodding through the hall with an indoor watering can in her hand. Not that she made a friend out of the ghost; Vera wasn't the friendly sort, really. And as for the hamadryads, apart from the occasional trick on Beryl, they were far less trouble now that their clock had been returned to the dining room. Although Griswold blamed them every time something went missing.

"I hope my project gets a reasonable mark," Oswin said to Gemma, as he packed it up, ready for school. "I wish I had time to re-build the Ghost-O-Meter. My teacher won't understand why I made it look like a toy gun."

Gemma eyed him as she used the edge of his desk as a bar while she practised her ballet positions. "I never knew brain boxes like you panicked when handing in homework," she remarked.

"Huh! Well, I am now! I forgot about marks when I started this. Whatever was I thinking?"

"You were thinking," Gemma reminded him, "of clearing my name, of making Beryl and Dad agree that the house is haunted and that I am not mad. Which," she continued with her thigh against her ear, "you have achieved, and I thank you for that." Their eyes met for an instant.

"Sorry! I forgot," muttered Oswin, adjusting his glasses.

"I'm not so frightened anymore," Gemma smiled, moving to a new position. "I can see a ghost without running down the passage screaming."

Oswin grinned. "Right! Do you think you'll ever become a clairvoyant like Patricia?"

"I shall sooner dance on point until I bleed!"

"Ugh!"

"That happens you know," Gemma explained. "Sometimes dancing on point can make you bleed. I think that's why ballet stars dislike jazz and tap dancers. They have the joy of dancing without the pain and distortion. Ballet is an old art and I've been thinking I may give it up when I've done my next exam and have more fun."

"Yeah!" Oswin leaned back on his chair. "You know, I had an amazing time with this project. I did what I wanted to do."

"Do you think you'll become a ghost hunter like Mister Westworth?"

"Nah! I mean it's a fascinating hobby and all that but I don't think there's that many ghosts about anyway."

However, two weeks later, the marks for Oswin's project came back. He poured over it as Gemma mouthed the tune to some jazz steps she was practising in his doorway.

'This is a *science* project. Next time try and keep to *proven scientific facts...*' the teacher wrote.

"Yeah, so you don't have to stretch your brain!" Oswin muttered, and read on.

"What a cheek!" he cried out moments later. "Gemma, listen to this: '...*You've achieved higher marks than this for previous projects, Oswin. However I've awarded extra points for effort and presentation, and for the recording of sightings, which was methodical and ordered.*' Well done there, Gemma! Now listen to this: '*The Ghost-O-Meter was an imaginative touch, but does it really work? There is something odd in the school utility room. Could you bring you equipment and clairvoyant cousin to investigate?*'"

About the Author:

Fiona lives just outside London with her husband and three children. She loves ancient history, mythology, folklore and especially all things Celtic. Her compassionate interest in people, her fascination with Britain's rich and colorful heritage, and her endearment to its picturesque land are reflected in her delightful storytelling.

 Fiona mostly writes fantasy and historical woman's fiction but also some children's fiction. When she's not penning stories in a nook beneath the stairs, you may find her cooking up a storm in the kitchen, reading tarot cards, or just doing household chores.

Visit her online at:
http://www.fionalaw.webs.com

More great books by Fiona Law:

Saint Alba's Jawbone
The Hand of Glory

Also from Eternal Press:

The Hand of Glory
by Fiona Law

eBook ISBN: 9781615722921
Print ISBN: 9781615722938

Fantasy Romance
Novella of 26,875 words

When two strangers request a hand of glory from the witch Briony, she is coerced into accompanying them to perform a sinister spell used by tricksters and thieves. Full of suspicion and prejudice, Briony takes with her a Vila imp for her protection.

To her consternation, Briony finds herself struggling against her attraction to the younger man, Gareth. She cannot possibly allow herself to fall in love with a thief, especially one who has the audacity to revile her lifestyle. Yet their mutual desire is too strong to be denied...

Until, too late, Briony discovers she has made a dreadful mistake. Can she undo the harm she has caused? Even if Gareth survives, could he welcome her into his arms once more?

Also from Eternal Press:

The Morning Afterlife
by Sonnet O'Dell

eBook ISBN: 9781615725687
Print ISBN: 9781615725694

Young Adult Paranormal
Long Short Story of 16,786 words

If remembering could bring about the end of everything, would you still try?

Karrin wakes up on the side of the road with selective memory loss; she knows her name and age but nothing more about herself. She walks the highway back to a town to find all but a few people have disappeared and that there are strange but beautiful beings hunting them down. It seems to her that some great apocalyptic event happened but she just doesn't remember it.

Karrin however is in more danger than she realizes as someone in her new group of friends is more deadly to her than those hunting them down. When she finds one of them, a young man roughly her own age named Gabe injured, she goes against all she's been told and helps him. Gabe in return wants to help her, help her to remember. Karrin's memories, however, could put her in even more danger and bring an end to everything she now holds dear.

CPSIA information can be obtained at www.ICGtesting.com
Printed in the USA
BVOW031111060312

284552BV00001B/13/P